REVEAL

Among Us Trilogy book 3

ANNE-RAE VASQUEZ

Developmental editor
JOSEFINA ROSADO

Augmented Reality
PUBLISHING

A Truth Seekers end of the world religious thriller series

Book 3 in the Among Us Trilogy. Copyright © 2018 by AR Publishing Anne-Rae Vasquez.

www.amongus.ca www.anne-raevasquez.com

Developmental Editor: Josefina Rosado

Editor: Danklerr Benadam

Cover graphic by Vanesa Garkova

ISBN 9780992145873 AR Publishing – Amazon Print Edition

❀ Created with Vellum

For Joseph, whose vision and support inspired me to write this book. For my kids, who inspired me to learn about the hidden talents of online gamers. For my parents who always supported my creative madness.

For Josefina, who continues to push the borders of my creativity to help me bring Harry, Kerim, Cristal and Serena to life. She is the best book doula and developmental editor an author can ever have.

Finally, for you, my Truth Seekers who dared to believe.

CONTENTS

PART III
THY KINGDOM COME

Note from the publisher

If you haven't read *Doubt book 1 and Resist book 2 of the Among Us Trilogy*, we highly recommend you do so before continuing. We've provided you with a plot summary of book 1 and a list of Characters at the end of the book for reference.

PROLOGUE

LIMBO

Ayear passed. The instability caused by the global earthquake of 2013 brought numerous uprisings and invasions. The Ebola virus wiped out tens of thousands of people in the US, and hundreds of thousands across Europe, Asia and Australia. During this time, the international offices of Global Nation served as provisionary governments for each nation.

"Mankind has really gone mad!" Carlos said, waving his hand. "A Nobel Peace Prize for Aaron? He's gaining more followers calling him the Savior!"

Bina looked up, the images from the world of the living were playing out on the smooth water's surface of the pool. She shifted her weight on the stone ledge, her gaze going past him, across the yard to the house.

She was picturing how Harry looked, the last time they were together. She heaved a tired sigh. The moment with him was brief—too short for a mother to enjoy with her only child.

Watching his life unfold in the reflection pool was the only connection she had left with him after her multiple attempts at contacting him. Was he ignoring her and if so, why? The doubts in her mind left her feeling empty.

Carlos snorted, bringing her back from her thoughts.

"Look at how mankind is eating out of Bezel's hand! Why is God letting this happen?" He pounded his hand on his knee.

Unwilling to add to Carlos' tirade, she touched the water, changing the coordinates, the images now picking up the video feed from the GN network. Her face lit up when she saw the images of Harry with his arm around Serena.

"Shush. They're replaying Harry's wedding anniversary bash," she said.

Carlos replied, "Such good news to hear that Lionheart appointed Harry to be GN's top political advisor and Serena to be the Communications Secretary."

She nodded, knowing he was going off on another of his political mantras. She shut out his words, focusing on the images in the pool.

"...and it's just hilarious that Lionheart doesn't know that Harry is the leader of the resistance! The very movement that she is trying to destroy." His laughter filled the air and echoed into the courtyard.

The image was now of Serena, Harry's wife, standing at the podium addressing the people.

Carlos wagged his finger. "GN needs to get the youth vote. I guess that's why Lionheart has poor Serena delivering GN's messages now."

Bina threw him a frown. "Hush. I want to hear what she has to say."

His eyebrows shot up as he glanced over to her.

She hunched over, focused on the speech.

"Good evening, fine citizens," Serena said, "As you may have heard, arrests are under way as we speak for those who choose to disobey the new orders. The detainees will remain in an undisclosed area until they have been rehabilitated and safe to re-enter society. Do your due diligence and stand up for America by standing in line for your microchip. It will save your life. Together we will make the United States of America, the powerful country it once was."

Carlos snorted again. "What a bunch of bull!"

Bina gave him a glare. "Hush!"

He pressed his lips together and nodded.

"...health care and food rations are determined on the basis of the data we receive via the microchips. More rations will be delivered in the next scheduled mail drop day in your area."

Bina shook her head and sighed. "That's enough. I'm sick of this."

Carlos leaned forward and touched the water, the images now showing familiar streets. He knew that Bina enjoyed watching what happened in Megiddo, in the parallel world of the living.

He cleared his throat. "Aaron Doub or someone who looks exactly like him was seen in the streets of Megiddo."

Bina frowned. "Oh?"

"But Walid knows better than to let the real Aaron out on the streets, right?" he asked.

Bina fell silent. She had contacted Walid on several occasions, giving him instructions on how to keep Aaron in hiding. She made him believe that the real Aaron Doub was part of a witness protection program and that Bina was a secret agent.

He never questioned why she only appeared at his home, and for that she was grateful. It was the easiest place for her to appear to him as a living person. It was the parallel version of where she and Carlos lived where both worlds overlapped.

Bina touched the water, this time bringing images that she knew Carlos dreaded seeing.

Cristal lay on the ground in her ten by ten foot cell, her hair serving as a pillow. Apart from not having a bed, they treated her better than others imprisoned at GN Tel Aviv. GN guards gave her three meals a day, daily showers and a regular change of uniforms. But Bina knew that was of little comfort to Carlos.

He stood up and waved his fist. "Cristal! Can you hear me?"

His previous attempts at communicating with her were futile. And yet, he never gave up trying.

Bina got up and grabbed Carlos' hand. "At least, Bezel has given up asking her about where the real Aaron is."

He squeezed her hand, his body shaking as the sadness overcame him. "Will he ever release her?"

Bina drew him close to her, unable to answer.

He looked up to the heavens and cried out. "Raffe? You were supposed to protect her! You coward! How can you call yourself an archangel of God?"

A cold breeze blew across the surface of the water, the waves erasing the former images and replacing them with a new scene.

A man walking barefoot, dressed in red and white striped pajamas was wandering up a dusty street of small shops. He passed a young couple that turned to watch him.

Carlos muttered. "How can a grown man walk around on the streets like that in his sleeping clothes? And talking to himself, no doubt."

Bina's eyes widened. "He's not talking to himself. Look!"

She pointed at the grey shape that seemed to follow the man.

Carlos leaned forward. "Yes, yes, I see it."

Bina touched the water, the images zooming into focus. She gasped when the man turned. Despite the gauntness in his eyes and cheeks, his beak-like nose was a dead giveaway.

"It's Aaron," she said.

"Aaron? What is he doing outside wandering around alone?" Carlos cried out.

"He's not alone," she said in a quiet voice.

"What?"

"Gabriel is with him," she said.

"Why would Gabriel be with him?" He ran his hand through his hair and shook his head.

Bina turned to him, a look of confusion on her face. "Gabriel isn't the only one with him."

Carlos raised his eyebrows. "What?"

Bina shrugged her shoulders. "There is a man with a beard; he's wearing a white robe with sandals on his feet."

Carlos cut her off. "Aaron is wandering the streets with Gabriel and another ghost, identity unknown."

Bina put her hand up. "Wait a minute, I wasn't finished."

"Okay, finish," Carlos said, crossing his arms.

It was then that Bina smiled.

"There's an army of angels behind him."

PART I
DECEPTION
Global Nation Tel Aviv

Slipping in and out of both worlds
The land of the living
and the realm of the dead
Where do I belong?

AR Vasquez

CHAPTER 1
DR. GOLDBERG

Dr. Goldberg entered the room with a chart and a tray of vials for Cristal's routine psychiatric assessment and treatment.

"You know the drill, Patient 878. Remove your outer shirt," Goldberg said avoiding eye contact.

Cristal yanked off the grey sweatshirt and slung it on the chair. Standing in a tank top and track pants, the dank breeze from the air conditioning unit prompted goose bumps on her arms. Her triceps, biceps and quads were honed and lean, a result of nightly workouts and physical training after lights out.

Her eyes flickered to the doorway where a female GN guard stood watch. No demon signals from her bracelet meant she had the advantage—two humans inside and a third one outside the door. She could take them down and escape if needed.

The guard threw her a glare.

Cristal dropped her gaze to the ground. What held her back was the mission from the Almighty Himself which came above her own self interests. Raffe, aka archangel Rafael, had given orders on behalf of the Almighty to infiltrate Global Nation and send Bezel, aka the devil, back to the pits of Hell. Months into her incarceration, she achieved neither. The hope her Truth Seeker friends would save her from Bezel's wrath had all but faded.

As the months passed, plans for escape filled her thoughts. One was to teleport back to New York to join Harry and Serena. Temptation to flee was overruled by her desire to complete the mission and save mankind from obliteration.

"Stop fidgeting or this will take much longer than it has to," the doctor snapped, wrapping the blood pressure sleeve on her arm.

And so the testing began with a scribble in the notebook and then on to another test and more scribbling. Test, scribble, test and scribble.

"Dr. Goldberg, what's the diagnosis?"

The doctor's left eyebrow shot up. "The physical testing will be over soon. You can ask your questions in the next half of the session."

"Did anyone tell you how reassuring your bedside manner is, Doc?"

The doctor pursed her lips and turned to the guard. "Bring in the chair."

The guard held the door open while the other guard pushed the chair into the room.

Dr. Goldberg tapped her toe and sighed with impatience until the guard left the room. Cristal wondered whether the doc was more wound up than the hair bun perched on her head. Holding her notebook in one hand and a pen in the other, Goldberg plopped into the chair, her dark marble eyes peeking over her thick black-framed glasses.

"What is your name? Do you know how you got here?"

Cristal repeated in verbatim what Bezel had ordered her to say on the first day of her imprisonment. "I have no recollection of who I am or how I arrived at GN."

The doctor dropped her head; her glasses sliding down the steep slope of her nose. She scribbled a note and read out the next set of questions.

Cristal's mind wandered, her responses on autopilot. She tried to drown out the sound of the doctor clucking her tongue on the roof of her mouth as her pen scribbled away.

Every day, the same thing. Same questions, same answers and a bunch of scribbling. Bezel's mental torture sessions and Dr. Goldberg's redundant questioning would have driven an ordinary person to insanity. But Cristal was far from ordinary.

Breaking routine, Cristal launched some interrogation of her own.

"You speak English very well," she said in the friendliest tone she could muster.

The reply from Dr. Goldberg was a curt, "We must focus on you, not me."

She pressed on. "Let me guess. You probably grew up in the US, maybe even born there and now you've moved to the Promised Land."

The doctor's nostrils flared and her pale skin flushed a lobster red. "Like I said. I ask the questions and you answer them. Understand?"

"Of course," she replied. From her quick assessment Goldberg wasn't being much of a foe.

"Let's begin then."

The doctor coughed into her hand and shifted in her seat.

And then it happened. Goldberg went off script.

"Are you being held here against your will? Just blink your eyes for 'yes' or look down for 'no.'"

Cristal's jaw fell open. *Was this part of the test?* Other thoughts rushed through her mind. *Was Dr. Goldberg working with Harry to rescue her?*

Her eyes blinked 'yes' despite her instinct not to.

Goldberg's eyes widened. "I see," she said, the pen still poised in the air.

Cristal paused, realizing there was no going back. She leaned forward. "Can you help me?"

The doctor glanced down and shuffled papers. After an awkward silence, she cleared her throat. "I, um, will see what I can do."

Cristal reached out and grabbed her arm. "*Will* you help me?"

The doctor stood up, yanking her arm away. "Yes, yes, of course. Like I said, I'll see what I can do. Best we end this now."

Cristal glanced up at the clock on the wall. "But we still have fifteen minutes left."

Dr. Goldberg mumbled something, then spun on her heel and rushed out the door.

CHAPTER 2
SOUL SEPARATION PROGRAM
SSP

Harry raced towards the ledge of the rooftop and at the last second skidded to a stop. He looked down the five stories of the newly renovated building to the empty alley below. Lionheart assigned him as project director for GN's new social housing development project. Six months into it, his crew renovated two of the six buildings which now housed 100 families. Three other renovations were in early stages of planning.

He bent over to catch his breath.

"This is why you don't skip training sessions," a voice called out.

He glanced up. Across on the next rooftop, Serena had her hands on her hips and a cute smirk on her lips.

"Do you want me to come get you?" she asked, swallowing her giggles.

He deserved that.

"Okay, Mrs. Doubt. You're not helping here."

"Okay, darling," she said in a singsong voice. "You can do it. You know I believe in you."

That did it.

He stepped back, jogged to the edge and leaped over the alleyway. He shut his eyes and landed hard on the tarred surface, sprawling face first.

"How's it going, Mr. Doubt?"

His eyes flickered open. Serena's black Parkour running shoes were in his field of view.

"I don't want to hear it," he said, pushing himself off the ground.

"Where's your sense of humor?" Serena leaned over with an open hand.

He gave a sigh, grabbed her hand and pulled himself up.

"I'm sick of Lionheart's broken promises. We should've been at GN Tel Aviv months ago."

She wrapped her arms around him. "And that's why..."

"And that's why we're heading to Tel Aviv tonight." He touched her cheek and placed his lips on hers, kissing her softly.

"Not much time. Let's get going," she whispered in his ear.

He smiled. "Lead the way."

She giggled. "What would you do without me?"

"I'd be nowhere without you," he said but she already turned and was sprinting to the opposite ledge.

"That's my girl," he said under his breath.

As Global Nation high-ranking senior officials, they had high-level access to classified data—data he previously had to hack to get at. For months they searched the databases looking for Cristal. When they couldn't find her in the Israeli GN RFID database, they searched through the restricted patient files.

The files didn't reveal patients' names, only their diagnostics—all were comatose. No big surprise.

Demons needed humans to participate voluntarily in the classified GN Soul Separation Program. In order to achieve this, Global Nation devised a fake news media campaign around a covert weaponized mutated measles virus called SSP, subacute sclerosing panencephalitis, formerly referred to as Disease X. According to GN Disease Control, SSP caused progressive brain inflammation leading to comatose states for those infected.

In 2015, GN accused the Chinese government for releasing SSP on American soil by soldiers disguised as university international students. China denied all claims and retaliated against the false propaganda by ejecting GN staff from the country, cutting all ties with Global Nation countries and isolating themselves from the world.

Subsequently, Ebola broke out in South Asia infecting and killing millions. The disease spread at an unprecedented rate reaching mainland China in a matter of weeks. When the Chinese death toll rose to the tens of millions, GN offered China a vaccine treatment to stop the spread of the disease. Faced with no alternative, China accepted the offer and soon after the government collapsed. As it did with other nations after similar outbreaks, GN stepped in to stabilize the situation and mitigate the economic and health crisis.

By the end of 2015, global populations began showing

signs and symptoms of SSP—mental deterioration, personality change, seizures and coma. Across the world, faced with disasters and SSP pandemic disease, governments fell to Global Nation's authority.

In response to the SSP outbreak, GN quickly set up quarantine and treatment facilities in all countries. Desperate for a cure, civilians infected by SSP registered for treatment and became unwitting test subjects for GN's covert operation— aka "Soul Separation Program."

By early 2016, under the guise of stabilizing nations from disease outbreaks and disasters, Global Nation controlled the world, managing all media outlets, the Internet and all forms of transportation. Martial law was imposed in every nation, restricting citizens from movement and communication with those outside their registered cities. GN had earlier grounded all air craft following the big earthquake claiming electromagnetic pollution in the atmosphere. Small pockets of resistance were quashed when GN transformed airports, train stations and ports into hostels or quarantine facilities.

Harry relied on his secret underground *interranet* to contact other Truth Seekers around the world. He and Serena reached out to their contacts in Israel searching for Cristal's whereabouts. After months of searching, the results remained unchanged. No one had seen or heard from her in months.

Then one day while scanning the GN Tel Aviv patient database Harry came across psychiatric assessments by a Dr. Goldberg for one comatose patient—the anomaly he was looking for. Why would a comatose patient need psychiatric assessments?

"The clock is ticking, Mr. Doubt!" Serena called out,

looking over her shoulder. "Are you coming?" She leaped onto the next rooftop.

Focus on the extraction mission.

"Right behind you," he replied.

CHAPTER 3
BEZEL

Cristal was trying to collect her thoughts when the door swung open. Bezel entered, gliding into the empty chair that Dr. Goldberg had just left. She sensed his presence earlier when he was in the elevator on the top level of the building. Her senses were constantly picking up overlapping imminent dangers. Just like troubleshooting programming issues, she blocked everything out and prioritized next steps.

Bezel, aka the devil, was adept at impersonating Aaron Doub, the appointed president of Global Nation and president of Israel. From conversations between the guards, Cristal learned that Israelis either tolerated or accepted his eccentric behavior. During a time of global devastation, the world needed a savior and President Doub fit the bill.

Unlike former Israeli presidents, Doub's physical appearance reflected his flamboyant personality and monarch-like persona. He held his head high with his crooked nose pointed upwards. Crowning his bald spot was a ridiculous comb-over sprayed with a high gloss finish. Adorned with tailored outfits cut with the fashionable "before the earthquake" look—broad shoulders, cinched waist, pencil thin pants and high-end pointed leather shoes, the fake president was a striking contrast to the rest of the population mandated to wear GN attire—army fatigues for military personnel, GN uniforms for workers and grey track suits for regular citizens.

"Let's forget the niceties and get to business," Bezel said.

His dark energy was already snaking its way around her head scanning her thoughts and memories—prying them from her mind. At least that's what he thought.

The mental probing would have been intolerable if Raffe had not trained her well.

Raffe's voice replayed back in her head.

Don't let the devil in. Fill your mind with happy memories or create fake ones. Build a world inside your head to drown out the real memories, especially the memories that could jeopardize the welfare of those connected to you.

"Now, you know I detest this part," Bezel said in a matter-of-fact way, squeezing his fingers into a fist.

She clenched her teeth as the sharp blistering pain ripped through her chest, pushing away the temptation to summon her powers to blast him back to the hole he crawled out of.

"You can't seem to stop for someone who hates it so much," she said through clenched teeth.

He relaxed his hand, easing the pain in her chest. "You cannot fathom the number of souls I have tormented over the expanse of time in the place humans call Hell. I am exhausted by the role I have had to play. All I want is to enjoy the wonders of humanity. Do you not think I am incapable of torturing you physically until you beg me to take your soul?"

He spoke in a low hypnotic tone and yet she sensed the tiredness in his voice.

"I believe you," she said.

In the last few weeks, Bezel let his guard down allowing the human vessel he possessed, Israeli special agent Yaffa, to replace the appearance of Aaron Doub.

Cristal's gaze panned away from the plastered white wall, past the stainless steel toilet and sink in the corner to the mat on the cold tile floor. Lights out was in five minutes. *Why was he here so late?*

He raised his hand turning his palm to her.

A black tattoo of a hexagram with an eye in the top triangle took shape. The same symbol printed on the back of US dollar bills called the Eye of Providence was associated with the Illuminati, a secret society conspirators believed controlled world affairs.

Why was it on his hand?

Bezel spoke in a soft but commanding tone. "Look into the eye and see for yourself."

Mesmerized by the intricate detail in the tattoo, she stared at the rays of light emanating from the eye.

Did it blink?

"Stop," she tried to say. Something was crawling up her neck. Her first instinct was to swat it but her arms hung like weights by her side.

"You need to see for yourself what the Almighty will not show you."

The eye widened just then and a burst of flames erupted from the center of the pentagram forming a ball of fire that grew to the size of a beach ball and continued expanding at a rapid pace.

The entire room lit up in flames. She stood in the burning inferno unaffected by the blaze.

Bezel sat motionless, the flames swirling around him as his appearance transformed back and forth from Aaron Doub to special agent Yaffa.

Cristal tried to grasp what the fire show was all about when a vision appeared before her.

In the vision, there was an ocean filled with fire. Swimming between the flames were thousands of men and women reaching out for help. Their bodies, a translucent collection of blackened ashes, rushed upwards and fell back into the inferno in an endless cycle. If that weren't enough, the smell of burning meat laced with the stench of rotten eggs and the desperate pleas for help triggered a wave of nausea in her gut. Air, she needed air.

Why couldn't she turn away from these horrifying images?

It dawned on her that she was watching human souls desperately trying to climb out of the sea of fire.

A black cloud hovered over the outstretched hands and soon scattered into thousands of winged bat-like creatures, charred black with blood red eyes. They swarmed above lashing at the souls with their claws.

Dear God, I can't take this anymore. She whispered the special words for teleportation, "Bo nelech" (which meant 'Let's go' in Hebrew) just as she had done the night of the exorcism. Like that night, the words did not take her away.

"That's enough," Bezel said. He dropped his hand, breaking the spell.

In an instant, the abhorrent images of Hell vanished, leaving Cristal's nerves in knots. Her heart was beating a mile a minute, but she forced herself to remain calm.

Breathe, Cristal, breathe, she could hear her father say. His voice soothed her every night. It crushed her to not let him know she could hear him. She didn't want to risk disclosing his location to the spiritual forces.

She took a deep breath. "If that was meant to threaten me, then you've succeeded," she said weakly.

He gave her a tired smile and stood up. "I need not threaten you or anyone. As I've told you, I'm here on Earth to learn about humanity. I want to understand mankind and what makes you who you are. The Almighty always favored humans over his angels. I am curious as to what makes your kind more special; I want to know why you are so unique. I do care about you Cristal Hernandez."

She swallowed the bitterness in her throat. "You have a funny way of showing it," she said.

He raised an eyebrow, surprised by her response but then resumed his cool demeanor.

"That's it for today. I am off to perform presidential things." He chuckled as if inviting her to chuckle with him.

"Can I ask you something?" she asked.

His lip curled into a small smile. "Ask."

"If you want to learn about being human, maybe you can cut all the daily interrogation and torture. Just talk to me. You know, like a regular person."

Bezel's fingers closed into a fist.

She held her breath, praying he would take her offer.

The cold expression on his face switched to a smirk. "I like that suggestion. From now on then, we talk one human to another."

"Then it's a deal," she said, letting out a sigh.

"Ah, yes," he said, "Making deals is my specialty."

She forced a smile and nodded.

He walked over to the door and paused, glancing back at her.

"I forgot to tell you..."

She swallowed hard, the smile frozen on her face.

"You may encounter some visions in your dreams. It is the side effect humans experience when seeing the Sea of Eternal Damnation."

Her stomach churned, but she fought to remain calm. "Yeah, thanks for the heads up."

His brow arched. "Heads up?"

She tried hard to sound pleasant. "Just a saying, President Doub. It means 'thanks for letting me know'."

"Ah, yes. You're proving to be very resourceful. By the way, I'm having a TV installed in here. Call it a thank you gift."

With that comment, he pulled open the door and walked out.

She let out a long sigh. Her knees wobbled as she got up from the chair. She braced herself against the wall, pressing her face against the cold cement. Two words ran through her mind: safe place.

Dear God, I know I shouldn't abuse this but please allow me to go to the safe place.

The familiar warm light embraced her. She closed her eyes as she drifted for a moment, welcoming the peace and serenity that surrounded her. There was music, more beautiful than any music she had ever heard on Earth.

"I'm here," a familiar voice said.

Her eyes flickered open.

Kerim stood before her, his eyes shining a silvery blue

grey. He was there and yet he wasn't; his body shimmering in and out of translucency.

Tears welled up in her eyes as the pain and anguish shook her body.

"I don't know if I can do this any more."

"You must stay strong, Cristal," he said.

How she missed hearing him say her name. But there wasn't time to be sentimental. She needed information.

"Where exactly are we? Is this Heaven?"

"We are on the outskirts of Heaven," he told her, "where each angel has their own place to heal before returning to battle."

"But I'm not an angel."

"The Almighty made an exception."

"Exception?"

He nodded, his grey eyes piercing hers. "You are the exception."

Why didn't that comfort her?

"Is this our safe place?"

He said in a quiet voice, "No, only yours."

A cloud of disappointment fell over her. She could hear his thoughts and she was sure he could hear hers. He wanted to be her guardian angel. She knew it wasn't going to be. Before she could say anything, he was gone.

CHAPTER 4
NEWS

The TV was installed as promised and Cristal left it running throughout the day. Most of the programming was local news filled with footage of President Doub and his entourage. Sometimes there would be back-to-back full feature Hollywood style movies starring former big actors. The movie storylines were laced with subtle GN propaganda messaging. Despite this, it was better than staring at the blank wall.

She had awakened in the early hours of the morning plagued by insomnia. At least she could entertain herself by watching TV. After an hour of repeat news programming, a feature film called Israel Impassible, starring Tom Cruise as president of Israel came on. Cruise resembled nothing like the real president except for the huge toothy smile and the manner he delivered his speeches, remarkably in fluent Hebrew, full of blustery empty promises and grand standing.

Voices outside the door interrupted the few moments of relaxation. GN guards entered the room.

The one with the baby face, dark wiry hair and a short wide build was called Noa. The taller awkward one with a permanent scowl was called Simcha, which in Hebrew meant joy.

The daily routine was consistent. The guards brought her meal at eight o'clock in the morning, standing inside the room while she ate. They would chatter to each other in Hebrew assuming she couldn't understand.

At noon, the guards would return with the lunch meal. After that, they'd escort her to the showers which meant passing the SSP Quarantine zone, a gymnasium sized area with floor-to-ceiling glass walls. Only special personnel were allowed inside but it was easy to see SSP patients sleeping soundly in their glass rooms. As months passed, the guards told her that new patients were coming in and the old ones were moving to the SSP treatment facility. She shuddered knowing the treatment facility was in fact the soul separation facility—the place where GN demon surgeons separated the souls of SSP patients to feed their demon patients.

Next stop would be the courtyard where she could walk around in the open air for ten minutes. Aside from the chain-linked fence above, she enjoyed seeing the sky, still darkened red with orange streaks. She treasured these few moments outside, breathing in the balmy air while tiny beads of sweat sprouted on her arms.

One day when the guards escorted her to the showers, she heard Noa drop Harry's name.

Taking a chance, she asked in broken Hebrew, "What is the news on Harry Doubt? Is he coming to GN Tel Aviv?"

Noa's eyes lit up. "You speak Hebrew?"

Cristal said, "A little."

"He got married at GN New York."

She swallowed hard. "Married?"

"Yes! Oh, the bride is so cute too. What's her name, Simcha?"

"Selena," the older guard said.

"Serena," Cristal said without thinking.

"Ah, yeah. Serena. That's her name. How did you know?"

"Uh, the doctor told me." She scolded herself for the slip and hoped they would drop the topic.

The guards carried on, chatting openly about various interesting and not so interesting things—President Doub's latest speeches, gossip about the horrible food in the canteen, the way some GN higher ups would complain about their weekly reports and other work-related grief. Interesting topics around international and local news like the chip implant program, a requirement for all citizens, drew her attention. They showed her the scars on their hands from the chip insertions.

"You will get one too," Simcha said. "All the patients on this floor will get one once the GN Staff have gotten theirs."

"What's it for?" she asked.

Noa answered with a bright smile. "Help ration out the food and supplies and health care for everyone. It's a good thing. Means no one will go without food, shelter and medical support."

Simcha snorted. "Just a way for GN to track everyone. They know where we go all the time. If I go to bathroom, they know I am in bathroom."

Simcha's rough manner of speaking meant that Hebrew

wasn't her first language. Not knowing where she was from made it difficult to read her.

◈

ON THE ANNIVERSARY OF HER INCARCERATION, THINGS began much the same way as before.

The guard Simcha handed her a steel tray carrying a bowl of desert beige lumpy mush, a vague semblance of hummus. Wedged on the side of the bowl was a triangular piece of pita bread, dry and cracked—the usual grub.

Simcha elbowed Noa and said, "Can't wait for tomorrow."

Noa smiled. "Vacationing in Eilat. We better make the most of it!"

Simcha's smile looked more like a sneer. "Yeah, I heard David will cover for us tomorrow."

"Would be better if David came to Eilat with us," Noa said.

Simcha snorted. "Hah, he's just a boy."

Noa turned and gave Cristal a wink. "Don't listen to her. David is not a boy. He's a brave strong man. She just has a big crush on him."

Simcha scowled. "Hmpf! Crazy talk."

They continued arguing. She half listened, soaking the bread into the hummus.

Simcha lowered her voice, glancing at her sideways before saying, "He is big troublemaker. When patient 454 went missing, David was questioned."

Noa shook her head. "We all were questioned."

"Not the same. He was interrogated by the General himself." She rubbed her nose on her sleeve.

30

"Ah?" Noa raised her brow.

"Better not talk in front of 878." Simcha looked over at her with her chin raised.

Cristal dropped her gaze to the plate and with the scrap of pita mopped up the last of the hummus.

"Eh, what's the big deal? She's harmless. Right, 878?" Noa called out.

She raised her eyes. "Hm? What's up?"

Simcha gave her a wary look, reached out and grabbed the tray. "You are done now."

"Uh, okay," she said. What was with Simcha's sudden change in mood?

Noa looked just as surprised but she kept her usual busy tongue silent.

Simcha walked out the door with Noa following steps behind.

Cristal believed things were going to change. She wasn't confident on how but time would tell.

CHAPTER 5

FORBIDDEN

Darkness was falling fast and the curfew was looming.

"Keep up with me. Kerim's going to be onto us soon," Serena said, taking longer strides.

"He never said we couldn't cross over," he said, trying not to gasp for air as he picked up his pace.

She glanced over her shoulder. "He literally used the words 'I forbid you to go where both worlds cross.'"

"That's just *angel talk*. What's he going to do? Kill me?" He knew she didn't buy into his false bravado.

"I don't want to think about it. You finally got the guts to do this. No time for regrets."

They continued running in silence until they arrived at the border.

A large sign at the end of the road read, "Do not enter. Danger. GN authorized security only."

Serena slowed down to a walk. "We're being watched."

"We're almost there."

Those who refused to get RF chip implants hid in the abandoned buildings that remained amidst the destruction and devastation beyond the border.

Kerim and his guards patrolled the area outside the Rebuild Zone every night. Anyone out past curfew was hauled away to GN for rehabilitation.

Serena scanned the area and nodded to him with the all clear sign.

They walked past the border, observing what was around them. They were steps away from Gabriel's apartment, the portal where both worlds crossed.

Emotions and memories flooded his mind. The supernatural forces surrounded them. His bracelet didn't have to warn him. He could feel their presence waiting to swallow them up whole.

A soulful wail broke the silence.

Serena's expression grew dark. "We should've gone back to save her," she said.

"Serena," he said, reaching out to touch her shoulder.

"We waited too long," she said before stepping into the mountain of crumbled bricks.

"We had to be cautious to prevent..."

"... endangering Cristal's life. Doesn't make up for the fact that we abandoned her."

He knew she was right.

She stepped into the debris, her body dissolving into the portal. He picked up his pace and followed after her.

THE DANK SMELL OF OLD CARPET HIT HIS NOSE AS HE

stepped into the shadows of the lobby. Serena had sprinted ahead, swinging the stairwell door open.

She turned and raised her eyebrows. "Come on."

"I'm two steps behind you."

She smirked and stepped aside to let him by.

He reached out to hold the door. "Ladies first."

"Whatever," she said. She pulled out a flashlight, flicked it on and darted up the stairs. The light cast long shadows on the stairwell walls.

They raced up to the third floor, their steps echoing around them.

Serena reached the landing and opened the door.

"If you say, *Ladies First* again, you're going to get it," she said with a tiny grin.

He never could read her despite being married for a year.

"Is that a promise?" he said brushing past her.

"Don't push it."

They continued down the hallway. The crackle of the incandescent light bulbs, the orange carpet and the textured wallpaper were exactly as he remembered.

A wave of energy brush past him.

"Serena, hold up."

She lifted her arm, the orange glow from her bracelet catching his eye.

Vibrations rippled around his own wrist.

Serena gave him the signal to pick up the pace.

He raced down the hall. The walls of the hallway compressed and decompressed in sync with the vibrations. They had to get to the safe zone inside Gabriel's apartment fast.

Serena rushed to the door, scanning it for its weak spot.

She lifted her right leg and kicked the area below the door-knob with the sole of her foot. The door gave in a bit. She gave it two more sharp kicks before it gave way. She waved for him to follow and ran inside.

A high-pitched sound filled the air followed by the flapping of wings.

A deep voice bellowed. "I command you to stop!"

Nothing was going to stop him. With that thought, he stepped inside.

CHAPTER 6
CROSSING OVER

E verything looked the same as it did the day they crossed over. And yet everything was different. Something else was in the room with them. Harry couldn't see what it was, but he sensed it. The lights flickered and the edges of the walls bent inwards and outwards as if the room was breathing.

Serena stood in the middle of the room, her eyes fixated on the ceiling.

"What is it?" he asked.

Her mouth was open but there was no sound.

"Serena?"

He stepped towards her.

"Do not come any closer," she said in a voice that wasn't hers.

The tips of his fingers tingled and his joints throbbed. Whatever it was, he could not let it sense his fear.

"Leave Serena's body now. I command you in the name of

the Almighty God, our Father," he said in a firm voice. Ten months of spiritual warfare training had better pay off.

Serena's head tipped to the side and turned to him with a glassy eyed stare.

"That may work for someone of less significance but you're going to have to try harder." The voice that came from her mouth reverberated around the room.

This was the place where both the spiritual and human worlds crossed. Demons or angels wouldn't dare hurt them here.

"Or so you think."

Whatever was inside Serena cracked a sick smile.

"Don't pretend to know what I'm thinking," he said, keeping his voice steady. Demons would say or do anything to manipulate the situation.

"You dare speak to me like this?" the demon said in a monotone voice.

His heart raced in his chest while his mind tried to think of a smart comeback.

"Yes, I dare" was all he could say. Serena always had been better with the retorts.

The demon raised her arm outward, bending it at the elbow at an abnormal angle.

"Kneel and submit yourself to me or else I shall break your wife's arm."

His stomach twisted into a knot. *Can't let this thing figure out my weakness.*

"Why would you think that would make me kneel down to you? If you must know, our marriage is a sham. It's all a show for GN," he said.

"As you wish."

He watched in horror as Serena's arm flung back and snapped at the elbow.

His gut tightened despite his efforts to remain aloof.

"In the name of YHWH, our Lord our God, reveal yourself," he called out.

Demons preferred to hide behind their human vessels' identity, their anonymity giving them power over their spiritual rivals. His training had taught him that they could not refuse identifying themselves if called to do so in the name of the Lord God.

Serena's life was riding on this theory working.

Her body was contorting like a puppet, bending forward and backwards. Her life was in his hands. He had to take control of the situation.

He repeated in a loud voice. "In the name of YHWH, the Lord our God, reveal yourself."

White froth seeped out of her mouth followed by the sound of metal scraping metal.

"I am called Soraya," the demon cried out.

The room shuddered around them but he remained resolute.

Raising his hand, he pointed at the thing that hijacked his wife's body. "I command you Soraya to leave the human immediately, in the name of the Lord our God, the One, the Only, the Almighty."

Serena's eyeballs rolled back, showing only the whites. Her mouth fell open and the thing inside her erupted from her lips like green sewage. It spewed into the air and morphed into the shape of an animal, a cross between a bobcat and a wolf.

He watched Serena's body crumple to the floor. Every inch of him wanted to run to her. But it wasn't over yet.

"So what are you planning to do now?" the entity asked. The words gnashed together in his head like swords.

He had to get Serena to safety.

"We don't have a problem with you," he said.

Serena struggled to stand letting her injured arm hang to the side. He stepped forward, held her by the waist and helped her to her feet.

The dark shadow stepped aside. "You're right," it said. "I have no issue with you. In fact, we have been waiting for you."

Serena leaned towards him. "There's more of these creeps?"

Her voice was low, her breathing short and ragged.

"Ah, that's not very nice," Soraya said, "especially since you came here uninvited."

Several dark shapes stepped out from the surrounding walls.

Serena tried to step forward. He held her close to him, focussing his attention on Soraya.

"Like I said, we have no issue with you or your friends. Let us pass."

The demon spirits floated towards them.

Harry raised his hand, his palm facing outward. The energy inside him radiated from his core and out his limbs in waves. "I said, we don't have an issue with you. Unless you want us to."

Soraya raised her hand, a signal for the others to stand down.

"Mr. Doubt, do you think your weak threats scare me?" she asked.

Serena struggled to free herself from his grip.

"Probably not. But then again, demons are not known to be very intelligent," she called out.

The dark shadow opened its mouth baring fangs like daggers.

"This girl has no fear. She's either very courageous or suicidal," Soraya said.

Serena threw her a glare and moved forward.

"Stand down," he whispered, grabbing her arm.

She mumbled, "Roger that."

The creature Soraya slid closer, its mouth widening into a leery smile. "Like I said, we've been waiting for you. We both want something. Let's see if we can make this work for both of us."

CHAPTER 7
ABSURD

The plan started out simple enough. All they had to do was enter Gabriel's place and tap the ground to teleport over to Megiddo just as they had done when they had arrived a year ago.

Instead, here they were standing in his dead friend's apartment negotiating with a demon to let them pass through.

"Okay, you've got my attention," Harry said.

The demon creature stood on its hind legs and morphed into the shape of a woman.

"We want to help you send Bezel back to where he belongs," Soraya said.

He lifted his chin. "And who said I want to do that?"

She gave them a smile, licking her vampire fangs. "Your friend, the one you search for, let Bezel loose on Earth. Send him back and your friend will be free."

"You make it sound so simple," he said.

She floated closer to him, her hips swaying left and right.

Serena leaped in front blocking her with her good arm. "Don't come any closer!" she cried.

The demon shadows flew towards her in a swarm. She waved her arm to fend them back. "Get away from me!"

"Leave her alone!" he yelled.

Energy pulsed through his veins itching to release itself from his control. Keep calm. No need to start a war just yet.

The flock of demons swirled around Serena, slashing at her with their claws. She stood solidly on the ground. Her good arm blocked the strikes to her upper body while she used her kicks to deflect the strikes to her lower body. He could see an orange glow begin to radiate around her. Kerim had taught them how to control and unleash their supernatural powers. The demons didn't know what they were up against.

"Harry, shoot them!" she cried.

Energy surged through him. All he had to do was call it.

Serena turned to him. "What is taking you so long?"

A demon's claw swiped her cheek, leaving a bloody welt in its place. She whipped around and slammed the palm of her hand into its face, releasing a torrent of wild energy the size of a mini atomic explosion.

The demon howled as the atoms tore through its body.

Serena waved her hand in arcs, the orange light slicing the demons near her. They flew in irregular circles above, flapping their wings like a murder of crows. An opera of chaos with the maestro methodically blasting the demons one by one.

"Enough!" Soraya's voice cut through the howls.

The flapping sound of demon wings melted into sudden silence.

The few remaining demons sulked away into the shadows of the room.

Serena stood in a front stance with her left leg bent and the other leg straight, her hips and shoulders facing forward. She searched his eyes for a sign, anything to give her a reason to start blasting.

"Stand down," he said.

She gave a quick nod and relaxed her stance.

Soraya walked to the couch and sat down, opening her hand to him as if inviting him to sit beside her.

"Excuse my associates' horrible manners," she said. "They haven't been in the company of humans for a long time. Please let's start over."

Every single passing minute was becoming more absurd.

Serena watched him carefully.

He said, "We're fine where we are. Tell us what you have in mind."

The demon sat back, crossing her legs. "So it's going to be like that, is it?"

He clenched his fist. "Don't test my patience."

She flashed them a mouth full of incisors. "Patience is what you mortals know nothing about."

"As I said, let me know what exactly you have in mind or else we'll be on our way." He raised his hand, feeling the weight of the energy radiating from the fingertips.

Her lips parted and a snake-like tongue slid out. "I know you are aware of what's going on in the inner circle of the White House."

A lump began to form in his throat. "Not sure what you mean," he said softly.

"Do you think the group of humans you've been training

could do all their subversive deeds under Lionheart's nose without my help?"

"Is that all you have?" he said.

"Fine," she said, crossing her arms. "The recent outbreak of Cholera and Ebola wasn't an Act of God, so to speak."

He fell silent.

She continued. "Tell me who kidnapped President Roshenbaum."

"What?"

"Don't pretend that you don't know that your people are behind this."

"I don't know what you're talking about."

"My sources have video evidence of the vice president's role in the unleashing of man-made disasters and releasing of deadly diseases to specific target populations in America."

Her words echoed what evidence that he and Kerim had uncovered in the last few days. He glanced over at Serena who, to someone who didn't know her well, appeared unmoved by the conversation. But he knew the wheels inside her head were spinning.

Soraya placed her hands over her knee. "Roshenbaum had the wool pulled over his eyes by his lovely wife and his best friend, the Vice president. But you thought he was behind this so you had him kidnapped."

"Like I said. I have no idea about any kidnapping. I will say though, we did uncover the VP's role in the disasters and man-made devastations and are in negotiations with others to bring him and his network down. I am aware that we are also working with demon forces to achieve this goal."

"So you had no part in Roshenbaum's kidnapping? Are you implying that rogue human conspiracists are trying to get their revenge? Seems rather a thin explanation when the top two GN spokespersons are trying to escape this continent via supernatural means."

"...or maybe opportunistic rogue demons are staging a coup," Serena said under her breath.

Soraya flashed her a deadly glare.

Harry had to steer everyone back to the objective at hand.

"As I've said and will continue to say, we have nothing to do with the kidnapping of the president. But I am aware that he is one of yours. I also am aware that he wants to preserve the human race for his and your own self-interests. Whoever is behind his disappearance will be revealed soon enough since you and your associates will see to that, I'm sure." He took a step towards her. "Now, my colleague and I have a bigger mission at hand which all of us will benefit from if we complete it."

She watched him carefully. "You think you can bring President Doub down?"

He gave her a smile. "If anyone could do it, it would be me. I'm his son after all."

"No," she said with her eyes cast down. "You don't know what you're up against. President Doub is as much as your father as I am your mother. You're going to have to do better than that."

He heaved a sigh. "How about this? Since you can't travel over to where he is, we are the only chance you have to send Bezel back to where he came from."

She pursed her lips for a moment and then flashed him a smile. "Fine. You cross over to Tel Aviv and meet our human ally on the other side. He has access to the friend you seek. He can help you get her out of Bezel's prison."

"How do I know your ally is not going to stab us in the back?"

"My word isn't good enough?" she asked. Her toe bounced up and down with impatience.

"Not enough."

She gave a short sigh and raised her hand, pointing her finger in Serena's direction.

A streak of light shot out from her fingertip and hit Serena on her broken arm.

Waves of furious energy rushed to his open hand. "Soraya, I warned you!"

A hand on his elbow made him turn.

"Hold up. She fixed my arm," Serena said, raising her arm as proof.

He faced the demon.

She crossed her arms. "Is that enough of a good will gesture?" she asked.

He shrugged. "Sure. Works for me."

CHAPTER 8
TIME IS NOW

Staring into the darkness, she braced for another sleepless night.

"Be careful, Cristal."

Kerim?

She sat up and peered into the darkness. A shimmer of light manifested before her.

"It's not safe. Repeat a prayer to block out anyone listening in just as Raffe taught you."

Yes. Got it.

"Dear God, Grant me the serenity to accept the things I cannot change and courage to change the things I can and wisdom to know the difference." She repeated the prayer under her breath as she focused on Kerim's words.

"A new guard will be here when the sun rises. He will provide you with details of your mission. Okay?"

"The extraction is finally happening?"

"Remember that the Almighty is with you."

She reached out towards the light. "And you?"

The tips of her fingers tingled as the light wrapped itself around them.

"I am always with you. Now I must go."

She closed her hands into a fist. The light between her fingers melted into the darkness.

She felt herself sinking. She tried to open her eyes but realized they were open. The darkness was filled with shadows approaching her from all sides. She screamed, but no sound left her lips. She tried to run, but her legs remained still. The more she tried, the deeper she sank. A part of her was shaking with fear. The other was relieved that soon it would all end.

"Get that thought out of your head."

Her eyes snapped open.

Kerim?

She sat up, her heart thumping in her chest. It was another nightmare, the fifth one this week. She brushed the dried tracks of tears from her cheek and brought her knees to her chest.

When she reached out to Dr. Goldberg for help, the doctor and Bezel's visits ended. Coincidence?

Closing her eyes could mean slipping into another nightmare. She ran her fingers against the charms on her bracelet tempted to power it up.

"Do you even work anymore?" she asked the bracelet.

The charms began vibrating. A warm sensation washed over her and for the first time in months, she felt herself relax.

"Of course you do. What a silly thing for me to ask," she said with a small grin.

The globe charm began spinning. Whirring around and

around, the breeze from it tickled her skin. It was luring her to touch it. Pick any place on Earth.

The sound of young girls' laughter and the familiar smell of bread baking filled the air. She closed her eyes allowing the memories to flood her mind. Peace and warmth surrounded her and she welcomed it. It had been so long since she felt so safe.

"Tell her to stop!" a muffled voice cried out.

She shook her head. "No, please don't," she heard herself moan.

"I command you to stop at once," a deep voice said.

She tried to fight off whatever was trying to interrupt her short moment of bliss. A blast of light filled her head sending energy throughout her body in waves of scorching agony.

"Resist," she said to herself, pushing back with her own power.

"She's losing it," a familiar voice said. Her thoughts felt foggy as if something was erasing them.

What would happen if she didn't wake up?

"Leave me alone," she said aloud.

A commotion was happening but was it all in her head?

"We can't wait any longer. Today is the day," a male voice said.

She didn't understand what it meant. But she did recognize who said it.

"Gabriel," she whispered. Her eyes snapped open.

CHAPTER 9
ABU WALID

Under the cover of darkness, familiar shapes met her gaze—the table, chair, sink and toilet. There was no one else in the room.

It had been another nightmare, or more precisely a nightmare within a nightmare. She pressed her thumbs into her temples. The pressure did little to relieve the throbbing inside her head.

From the window in the door, the sterile white light spilled onto the floor like a welcome mat. The guards were about to arrive and she needed to collect herself.

A soft rap on the door broke the silence. Her gaze darted towards the door.

Another rap.

"Who is it?" she asked.

"New guard."

The guard's silhouette filled the glass window. She got to her feet.

"Okay, are you waiting for me to invite you in?" she asked.

She heard a grunt on the other side of the door.

"Yes," he finally said.

Guards usually entered unannounced. Her curiosity was piqued.

"Come on in," she said.

The door swung open. Shadowed by the darkness, the guard entered, pausing at the doorway.

"Wait. I open lights," he said in a gruff manner.

The guard held a tray of food. He reached for the switch, flooding the room with artificial light.

"*Bo-ker tov*, good morning," he said in Hebrew. When she didn't respond, he switched to Arabic, "*Kaif halik, bint?* How are you, girl?"

Her heart pounded as she tried to assess the situation. Simcha and Noa said that the new guard named David was just a "boy".

This guard was in his twilight years. His hair was a hornet's nest of silver and grey, contrasted by his cinnamon-colored skin. He gave her what was a half-sneer and a half-smile, the top row of his teeth half hidden by his top lip. Deep creases etched around his coal black eyes.

His beige army fatigues fit him snugly, stiff and wrinkle free. Oddly enough, he did not carry a rifle like the guards she knew. Instead he wore a black leather holster on his side.

After an awkward silence, he cleared his throat.

"My English no so good. You speak Hebrew or Arabic?" he asked.

"No," she said. Never let anyone know your strengths.

"Where's David?" she asked.

He placed the tray down on the table and pulled back the chair ignoring her question.

"Sit. Eat." He waved his large, ruddy hands towards the chair.

"Do you have a name?" she asked. She sat down and reached for the bread.

He gave a small nod and cleared his throat.

"You can call me *Abu Walid*, father of Walid," he said.

Her joints were humming with vibrations sensitive to the supernatural energy around her.

"I once knew a Walid," she said in a soft voice.

His nostrils flared slightly. She sensed her words hit a nerve.

He lifted his chin towards the tray. "Eat now, *bint*. We have long day ahead."

She tore a piece of the pita bread and dipped it into the hummus.

"Long day ahead? What exactly do you mean?" She put the bread in her mouth and chewed while observing his distinct mannerisms.

His bushy eyebrows shot up and was followed by a head tilt.

"You talk too much, *bint*. Finish your food."

Her joints began vibrating, the energy inside her, eager to reveal itself. If he proved to be a fraud, she toyed with the idea of letting her power loose on him.

"Why the rush? As you said, we have all day," she said, her gaze fixed on his.

He narrowed his eyes, letting his hand slide over his holster.

"I know not what you talk about. There is no time for this nonsense. Eat and act normal."

"Why? Are we being watched?"

He frowned. "I know not what you mean."

She ripped a piece of bread and soaked it into the lump of hummus. If this was the guard Kerim was sending to help her, why was he being so difficult?

She cast her eyes down on the tray as she ate. Was he going to stare at her all day? What was he waiting for?

She chewed on the last piece of bread. It was as gritty as sand but buying time was important.

The guard reached out and pulled the tray away.

"*Bekefeh*. Enough," he mumbled in Arabic.

"Hey, I'm not done yet," she said.

His face scrunched up into a scowl. "*Uskot!* Shut up!" he said, dismissing her with a wave of his hand.

She swallowed hard. "Excuse me?"

With a grunt and another wave of his hand, he turned to the door.

"*Mashnoona*, crazy girl. Too much work," he mumbled under his breath. He threw open the door and walked out.

She shoved the chair backwards.

Who was this strange person? Why would Kerim send him to her?

No time to analyze the situation. She ran out of the room after him.

CHAPTER 10
CLOSET

C ristal kept her distance behind the strange guard. From the look of things, he didn't even notice he was being followed. He was mumbling to himself and looking down at the ground as if he was searching for loose change.

She glanced into the other patient rooms as she rushed passed. More red flags. Every single room was empty. No patients, no beds.

Something big was going on. What were the chances she was walking right into an elaborate trap?

The guard came to an abrupt stop at the supply closet.

"They promise me a savior, instead I get a child," he said in Arabic.

He reached for the handle and paused, glancing over his left shoulder.

She ducked inside a doorway.

"We cleared the floor like you asked. You said that the one who will save us would be here," he said to the invisible person beside him. He paused for a moment as if he were listening. Then he said, "No, she is just a child. We are risking everything for this girl. Enough. You can take care of the rest yourself."

He turned back to the door, yanked it open and walked inside the room.

Energy was pulsating through her veins. Her bracelet was not sensing any supernatural entities. Things weren't adding up. What were the chances that this old guard was delusional and talking to the voices in his head?

The answers were behind that door.

She paused to assess the situation.

What if Bezel was behind this?

First option. Return to the room. Pretend nothing happened.

Kerim had told her to expect a new guard.

Second option. Follow this guy.

A cool breeze picked up from the ground and swept around her in circles.

"Have faith in the Almighty," her father's voice said in her head.

He was right. The one thing she needed now was to have faith.

"Dear God, help me," she said before opening the door.

Even with the light from the hallway, she couldn't see past the darkness inside. The darkness appeared to swallow her whole. Against her gut instinct, she stepped forward. Her foot smacked against a metal object. Something in it sloshed against the sides.

The door slammed shut behind her. *Oh geez.*

She reached over to the wall, searching for the light

switch. Wading into the pitch-black darkness, she took another step forward.

"Give me light," she commanded raising her arm.

Rays of white light shot out from the bracelet illuminating a few feet around her. By her foot was a janitorial mop bucket and wringer.

Where did that guard go?

She turned to the right and waved the light to assess her surroundings. The darkness was absorbing the light.

She kicked the bucket to the side, spilling soapy water on the ground.

The light bent in an arc, landed in the bucket and bounced straight to the ceiling like a blazing pillar.

She raised her arm to block the rays.

Voices filled the room.

"You have to go back there and get her."

Harry?

The deep voice of *Abu Walid* responded in Arabic. "What can that girl do that we cannot? I have been working on the inside exposing GN. Bezel trusts me as his right-hand man. I risk all this for an inexperienced child?"

"Soraya said that you'd help us," Harry said.

Who?

If *Abu Walid* was the ticket for her to get out of here, she had to convince him herself.

"Dear God, help me," she said.

Without further thought, she stepped into the light.

CHAPTER 11
WRONG TURN

Somehow she had assumed that stepping into the light would take her to Harry. Instead, she found herself inside another dark closet. This time, though, she wasn't alone.

A stocky man with olive colored skin, waves of dark oily hair and a savage expression on his face was leaning back against the metal storage shelves. Raffe. The last time she saw Archangel Rafael she had believed in the mission. Now not so much.

"Long time no see, Ms. Hernandez," he said letting his Israeli accent stretch out each syllable.

How could he be so calm after everything she'd gone through? And all for what? What good had it done for mankind?

"Raffe, is that all you can say? What is going on?"

He gave her a smirk. "Call it an extraction."

She shook her head. "I'm sorry. What? You left me in that cell for twelve months."

His thick brows knit into a frown.

"Twelve months in human time, is only a blink of an eye in universal time. Your mission was to build rapport with him. And you succeeded," he said.

She could barely contain herself. "Succeeded? Is that what you call it? What did this success gain for anyone? I thought I was helping save humanity and the spiritual world. By sitting in a cell for twelve months? Is that what you call progress?"

Her heart was pumping hard. She tried to slow her breathing. The frustrations built up during her confinement needed to be contained.

"Now, now. Didn't I train you better than this?" he said. He crossed his arms across his chest.

Angry words were ready to leap from her tongue. What good would they do? Play it cool.

She took several deep breaths until the wave of emotions subsided.

"Okay, so what's next?" she asked.

He cracked a small smile. "Good. Your next mission is to return to Megiddo."

Returning to Megiddo to be with Walid and his family was what she needed right now. She had replayed the memories of her time with his mother and sisters in her mind almost every night.

"Don't you think Bezel will notice I've disappeared?" she asked.

His smile morphed into a smirk. "You humans can't just take orders like good soldiers. If you must know, instead of all this talk, better I show."

He stepped back and pointed toward the ground. A spark of energy raced from the tip of his finger to where he was pointing and from that spot erupted a glasslike dome. The dome continued growing larger until it was five feet in height. During her spiritual warfare training, the domes, or what she nicknamed giant snow globes, was how he showed her live cams of places around the world.

Inside the giant snow globe were hundreds of people lining up at multiple queues to receive basic supplies. It resembled an airport check-in but instead of travellers bustling around the airport anxious to get onto their flights, people were dressed in matching grey jogging suits and filing in like inmates.

Raffe waved his hand. The scene zoomed in on one woman at the head of a line. Her shoulder length dark hair was peppered with grey streaks and hung limp against her hollowed cheeks. Her eyes were sunken into her face and her cheekbones jutted out like round oval stones. Cristal's heart sank.

"My mother?" she said under her breath. Without the pound of makeup and hair sprayed to perfection, she was barely recognizable.

"Watch," Raffe said.

The light panel flashed the number 17.

"Next!" the worker called out.

Her mother walked over to Station 17 and waited.

The worker perched on a tall stool, her stubby fingers two-finger typing on the keyboard. Every so often, she yanked at a bra strap that seemed to be cutting into her shoulder. The uniform hugged her body one size too snug squeezing her curves into rolls below her bra and above the waistline of her pants. Written in Hebrew, the name tag on her chest pocket said "Tirza" with the words "Global Nation Tel Aviv" underneath.

Cristal had seen enough. She turned to Raffe.

"Why is my mother in Israel?" she asked.

CHAPTER 12
OLIVIA BLOOM

Raffe crossed his arms and leaned back. He stared at her, debating whether to ignore or answer her question.

"I deserve to know," she said, her patience running short.

"Before the big earthquake, your mother went to Israel to find you," he said.

She wasn't buying that. Ever since her mother remarried, pleasing her husband was more important than being a mother.

"She didn't check in on me when I was at university so why now?"

The smirk crept back on his face. "Your stepfather left her for a younger woman."

She pictured the balding, short man with the beer gut romancing another woman. She winced at the thought.

"I highly doubt that. He knew he landed a catch when he met my mother. He put her on a pedestal."

"Believe what you want. Fact is, your mother left that excuse of a husband so she can find you."

Cristal turned to the globe.

The government worker said in Hebrew, "Stand still in front of scanner."

Her mother looked at the worker's name tag and said, "Ms. Tirza, I am an American. You work for GN so you must speak English, right?"

Her dad had always said that she inherited her stubbornness from her mother.

The worker scowled. "American?" she asked. She pointed to the body panel scanner and in stilted English said, "You know drill. Stand here."

Her mother moved to the scanner.

Something on the computer monitor caught the worker's eye. Her lips pressed into a thin line as her fingers flew across the keyboard.

"Something wrong?" her mother asked.

The worker continued typing. "Olivia Bloom, what is your purpose today?"

Bloom? Since when did her mother use her stepfather's last name?

"Picking up food and supplies."

The worker looked up.

"Our records show you were here seven days ago. You picked up your supply for this month."

Olivia gave a sigh. "Yes I did. Someone stole them at the hostel at GN Tel Aviv."

The worker typed on the screen. "Did you report this at GN?"

"Yes, of course I did. The lady at GN said that she entered

it into my chip. She told me to come back today to get a new supply."

Cristal turned to Raffe. "So she was staying at GN Tel Aviv this whole time while I was in confinement?"

He gave her a nod. "She believes the end of the world is near. She prayed to the Almighty to find you."

Now it was beginning to make sense. Her mother had always been very religious. It was possible that her turning to God may have driven her stepfather away.

In the globe, the worker stood up and motioned to her mother.

"Come with me," she said.

Two security guards moved in and stood on either side of her mother.

The worker tapped her finger on her ear and spoke. "We are bringing her in."

"What's going on?" she asked.

"We are taking you in for questioning, Ms. Bloom."

Just then, the snow globe went dark.

Cristal turned back to Raffe.

"The mission has something to do with my mother," she said. Her mother was never really close to her. Over time, Cristal had grown to accept it. Nevertheless, she was still her mother's daughter.

He gave a nod. "Yes. Mission is to extract Olivia. I assume you accept."

Many more questions came to mind.

"Do I have a choice?" she asked.

He shrugged. "The Almighty gave humans free will. So technically, yes."

"If I don't take on the mission, will her life be at stake?"

He raised his chin. "It's not about one person," he said.

"So you're saying many people's lives are at stake?"

His gaze pierced into hers.

She remembered watching the video where he told Kerim that humanity was on a downward spiral. That simple fact was why she could never trust him fully.

"What's the plan?" she asked.

"You will pose as Tirza, the GN interrogator," he said.

"Okay," she said. "Give me the run down."

Raffe took a step forward and waved his hand.

"No time. We must go now."

He hadn't changed one bit.

"What's the rush?" she asked.

Before she knew it, she found herself hurtling into the blackness.

PART II
ESCALATION

Tormented

Listen to the beat of the drum
The time has come

AR Vasquez

CHAPTER 13
MEGIDDO

With General Assaf refusing to finish the mission to bring Cristal to them, Harry and Serena were left to fend for themselves. Finding a safe house was the first thing on the list. Serena was quick to get in contact with her friend Walid in Megiddo. His uncle had a space for them—a tiny storage room in the back of his bakery.

Harry threw his hands up in the air. "What do you mean she disappeared?"

"Take it easy," Serena said, glancing up from the laptop screen. "I've checked the recordings from the security cameras on the floor she was on at GN. The camera feed ends before General Assaf enters the floor. It picks back up after we were in communication with him after entering the closet. The whole floor is completely empty."

He sat down on the chair across from her and began drumming his fingers on the table; a habit that he knew drove her bonkers.

Her eyes narrowed and her perky nose scrunched up into her "Do you mind?" look.

"Was Cristal the only patient on that floor?" he said, his fingers still thumping on the table.

She spun the laptop toward him. "Like I said earlier, the night before the floor had thirteen patients. Twelve were comatose and the other one was Cristal. Check it out yourself."

The display was split into twenty screens. One screen had a video feed for each room, hallways, common areas, shower room and elevator. The time stamp showed the date from the previous night starting at 9 pm. Outside the one room that presumably belonged to Cristal were two guards.

He bent over to look closer at the video's grainy picture.

He could make out Cristal lying on the ground with her back to the camera. Odd. The comatose patients all had beds.

"Did those GN bastards make her sleep on the ground?" he said.

"Take it easy," she said.

"Take it easy?"

"You know that mistakes happen when personal feelings distract you from the objectives."

She was using his own words to make her point.

"Keep checking the footage," she said.

He touched the monitor and selected all the video screens. He dragged his finger to scrub the video timeline forward.

At approximately 10 pm, one of the female guards enters Cristal's room. The lights in the room shut off a few seconds later. The guard comes out of the room and goes back to stand at her post.

He could make out Cristal's outline on the ground. Her body is motionless for hours. During the same period, the guards begin moving around the hallway and seem to be chatting with each other. The shorter guard appears to be telling a story. She waves her arms in the air, then turns and walks down the hallway with her head down as if she were searching for something on the ground. The other guard is laughing and pointing at her. Obviously an inside joke. At approximately 6 am, all the video feeds go black.

He scrubbed further to 8:26 am when the feeds picked up video images again. All the screens were now showing empty rooms and hallways. The whole floor had been vacated.

"Someone moved the patients when the video feeds went dark," he said.

"Except for Cristal. We know for a fact that the General spoke to her which was from 8 am until right before the video feeds come back up. He told us that he left her in the room," Serena said.

"The demons told us that General Assaf would get Cristal out," he said, slamming his fist on the table.

"Technically, he did get her out," she said.

He shook his head and said in a tone that came out sharper than he intended, "You're not helping here."

"I'm just as frustrated as you. Don't take it out on me," she snapped back.

She was right. Why was he being such a jerk?

Time to change the topic.

"I don't think I thanked you for finding us a safe house," he said, touching her hand.

She turned away. "You should be thanking our friend, Walid."

As if on cue, Walid entered the room. He had a rifle slung over one shoulder and was holding a cloth rice sack in the opposite hand. From the bag, wisps of steam and delicious smells of spicy meats wafted into the stuffy room.

"Hey guys, I find info you ask for," he said in broken English. He gave them a large toothy grin.

Serena grabbed the bag from his hand. "You're my hero, Walid. This beats energy bars and frozen meals."

Harry could swear that Walid was blushing two shades of pink.

She emptied the contents from the bag, pulling out baguettes filled with shawarma, cheese, and fresh veggies. She reached into the bottom and brought out a large thermos and a stack of paper cups and placed them on the table.

"What's in the jug?" Serena said grabbing a baguette sandwich for herself.

Walid chuckled, still blushing from her first comment, and reached for the thermos. He gave the lid a twist releasing a bitter aroma.

"Arabic coffee. Just what the doctor ordered," Harry said, reaching for a paper cup.

"My mother make best coffee," Walid said, pouring some into his cup.

Serena grabbed a cup and pushed it towards him, eager to have it filled. "I can't argue with you there. Your mom's coffee is awesome."

He placed the thermos down on the table after filling her cup.

"Eat with us, Walid," Serena said, pulling a chair back for him to sit.

Taking the invitation, he sat down and grabbed a sandwich. Before taking a bite, he said, "My guys at GN said that it's lock down there. Some guards who work on secret level said they are trying to find out who kidnapped the sick people on that floor."

Harry let Walid's words sink in, seeing if they correlated with the video evidence.

"The guards from that floor are being questioned by the president himself."

Harry shot Serena a look.

"Where did you get your intel? Did you go to GN Tel Aviv today?" Serena asked.

In a lowered voice, he said, "No, I talk to my contacts by secret *interranet* and cell network you and Mizz Creestal helped me build. Now we communicate with no GN listening." He paused and said, "By the way, how is Mizz Creestal? Why she not come here with you?"

Harry flashed Serena a look. Was Walid someone they could trust?

She blinked once giving him the all clear. That's all he needed to see.

He turned back to Walid and said, "Cristal was one of the patients who went missing at GN."

Walid's smile disappeared. "*Aasaf*, sorry. I did not know."

Serena patted him on the shoulder. "We need to find her and we're counting on you to help us."

"*Akeed*, of course, Mizz Serena," he said.

She leaned towards him. "You need to know that helping us could put you in grave danger. Do you understand?"

He blinked and nodded. "*Fahem*. I understand. I protect my family and my friends. My father and brother Sami disappeared after the earthquake. My mother told us that they are dead. But I think she believes this because she cannot accept the truth. This world has many dangers everywhere."

Serena shook her head. "I'm sorry to hear about your missing family. My mother went missing years ago which is why I joined the Truth Seekers to search for her."

His eyes lit up. "I always want to become Truth Seeker."

She grinned. "Well then, I shall nominate you to become a Truth Seeker."

Harry clasped his hands together and said, "I second the nomination."

Serena patted Walid on the shoulder. "Well then, Walid, you are now officially a Truth Seeker."

Walid's eyes widened. "Like the Truth Seekers' game? Sami and me used to play this all the time. But how can I be real Truth Seeker? Zero Doubt is only one who can recruit."

Serena pointed to Harry. "He is the one who recruited you."

Walid eyes darted to Harry and back at Serena while his smile stretched from ear to ear. "*Anjiad?* Really?"

Harry grinned. "Do you accept the invitation?"

"*Akeed!* Of course! I accept Meester Zero."

Time was marching on and the mission to save Cristal was at hand.

"Okay, enough of the chit-chat," he said. "We've got work to do."

CHAPTER 14
REUNION

Teleportation should be like riding a bike, she reasoned to herself. If that were the case, why did her body feel like it was being ripped apart?

A whooshing sound filled her ears and a blaze of light flashed around her. Gravity yanked her downward in a free-fall. The darkness melted away and she braced for the landing.

Float. Focus on floating.

Cristal's feet dangled in the air for half a second and then touched the ground. Touch down.

"Not bad," she whispered to herself.

A quick scan of her surroundings revealed that she was in another closet. She took in a deep breath.

"My apologies," a deep voice said from behind her.

She spun around and met Raffe's raised brow.

"Can you stop doing that?"

He tilted his head, giving her that annoying look of smugness.

"As I was saying, my apologies."

"What are you apologizing for?" she asked.

"Human fragility. Your human body cannot travel as fast as angels," he said.

A muffled sound interrupted their conversation.

Cristal glanced in the direction of the noise.

In the corner of the room was a woman, blindfolded, gagged and tied to a metal shelving unit. On her shirt, the name tag read "Tirza."

"Silence her," Raffe said.

Cristal's gut twisted into a knot.

"Go on," he said. "This is what you signed up for."

Spiritual warfare or any form of violence repulsed her. He was right though. She had no choice but to follow orders.

The GN worker moaned and thrashed, shaking the shelving unit and toppling cleaning supplies on the ground.

Cristal marched past Raffe towards Tirza. Being that the worker was human, she was restricted to only using her physical strength. She didn't know what was worse, hurting someone with her super powers or her fists.

She swung her arm and gave the woman a straight punch. Tirza's head snapped back.

She turned around. "Okay, she's silenced. What next?"

❧

TRANSFORMING INTO THE DOPPELGÄNGER OF TIRZA WAS already proving to be a pain. Cristal tugged at the uniform.

78

Could it be any tighter? All the places she was physically supposed to be able to bend were, let's just say, unbendable.

"It's show time," Raffe said in her ear.

"Got it," she said.

Cristal pushed open the door to the questioning room.

Her mother sat at the small wooden table with her back straight and head held high. Her strength was hiding the fragile mess she'd become. Bruises on her cheek and dried blood on her lips, evidence that Tirza and her goons had started the interrogation.

Stay in character.

"Ms. Bloom," Cristal said, deepening her voice and adding the best Israeli accent she could muster.

Olivia sat still as a statue.

Cristal did a quick scan of the room. On the far wall was a closed circuit camera.

"Ms. Bloom, we're moving you into a holding cell."

Her mother responded by dropping her head to her chest.

Raffe entered the room. Transformed into a clone of the GN guard he had thrown into the closet moments earlier, he was now half a foot taller and a hundred pounds heavier.

"Moshe," she said using his code name. "Get Ms. Bloom out of here."

"Come with me," he said.

Olivia got to her feet, swayed for a moment, then fell back into her seat.

Raffe grabbed her by the arm. "Come on. Stand up."

Her mother raised her arm to her face and pulled away. When she turned her face, Cristal could see tears crawling down her cheeks.

"Ms. Bloom, please. I don't want to have Moshe work on

you again," she said, motioning towards the door.

Her mother nodded as if resigned to accept her destiny.

Raffe grabbed her by the arm, yanked her up on her feet and shoved her out the doorway.

Cristal followed and swept her gaze down the hallway. Three GN guards and five GN staff were headed in their direction. The joints in her hands began throbbing. It was a disconcerting but familiar sensation—Bezel was close by.

Raffe turned his head. He gave a sharp nod for her to pick up the pace.

"Come on, Ms. Bloom, you can walk faster than that," she said.

Her mother pulled her arm away. "I'm not going anywhere."

What was going on here?

"Ms. Bloom, start moving or else you'll be facing more than detention," Raffe said pointing his rifle.

"No," Olivia said. "You promised that I could see the president. I'm not going anywhere until I do."

The president? What did she want to see him for? And why would Tirza and GN staff consider her request?

Up ahead people were stepping to the side clearing the path.

"President is en route," Cristal said.

Raffe eyed the supply closet on the right.

She took that as a signal.

"Of course, we are taking you to see the president right now," she said in a reassuring tone.

She hip chucked her mother towards Raffe who opened the door and shoved her inside.

Cristal slid into the closet behind him.

CHAPTER 15
MOTHER

In less than twenty-four hours, she'd been in three closets, had teleported twice, and here she was sitting in Walid's mother's kitchen watching her long lost mother sipping a cup of aniseed tea with Raffe back in his human form wearing a flowery apron and chopping onions at the counter.

Cristal heaved a sigh.

"It isn't right to be in Walid's house uninvited," she said.

Raffe looked over his shoulder. "You think this is the first time I've done this?"

Interesting to know Walid's home was a regular stop for this archangel.

He cracked a sly smile. "Do not worry. This family did not awaken even through the most recent Seven Archangel emergency assembly."

She turned to her mother. "What did you want to talk to the president about, mom?"

Her mother reached out and touched her hand. "Cristal, didn't I always tell you how powerful faith in God is?"

Cristal nodded. Suppressing the emotions, conflicting as they were, was how she'd have to deal with the reality that her mom was back in her life.

"You didn't answer my question," she said.

"Be polite. Don't talk to your mother like this," Raffe said. "Let your mother be glad; let her rejoice who gave birth to you."

He picked up two eggs and cracked them into the frying pan with one hand.

"Proverb 23:25," her mother said softly.

"What was that?" he asked as he grabbed a plate from the shelf.

Her mother replied, "Your quote is from the Bible."

He gave a loud snort and said under his breath, "You humans amuse me so."

The puzzled look on her mother's face was priceless.

Cristal leaned over. "Let it go, Mom," she whispered.

Her mother pressed her lips into a thin line.

Raffe spun around holding out two empty plates. "Ladies, you will have honor of my own special *shakshouka*, fried eggs and tomatoes."

Her mother clasped her fingers around the cup and said, "Thank you, Holy Archangel Rafael."

"Seriously mom?" Cristal wanted to gag. "Can you please stop calling him that?"

Raffe chuckled, enjoying the attention.

"Olivia, my dear child," he finally said in a solemn tone. "You may address me simply as Raffe."

Her mother gave an uneasy smile. Cristal knew that her

mother was still having a hard time dealing with the fact that she was talking with a real-life angel.

"Uh," her mother said, "Archangel, Sir."

Raffe placed the plates on the counter. "Call me, Raffe, please. Don't want to blow my cover," he said with a silly smirk.

Her mother gave a small nod. "Of course." She paused, casting her eyes briefly down to her teacup before saying in a small voice, "Raffe."

Cristal felt her insides twisting and untwisting into a Chinese knot. Watching Raffe and her mother carry on like teenagers on their first date was like reliving the courtship between her step-father and mother. Except this time was triple nauseating.

"I haven't eaten a hot meal since before the earthquake," Olivia said. "The food at GN was never fresh. We knew that animals had either died or disappeared when the earthquake happened. There was a rumor going around that GN scientists were busy in their labs making cloned animals and creating GN modified food. I wanted to confront the president with this."

Raffe said, "You just realized that now?" He went to the stove and began adding spices into the pan.

"Walid's mother grows her own vegetables and has her own chicken coop," Cristal said.

Her comment must have sparked something. Her mother flashed her 'I'm all ears' smile, sat up and leaned towards her.

"Really?" she asked. "From what I heard, after the earthquake the drought destroyed most of the farming land and yet you have running water."

Raffe turned to them.

How much was she allowed to reveal? Cristal shot him a look.

From his laissez-faire smile and the nonchalant way he stirred the wooden spoon, he didn't appear too concerned that her mother was asking way too many questions.

"GN set the sensors to only give two ounces of water," her mother said as she stood up and hurried to the sink. "May I?"

Raffe shrugged. "Be my guest."

Olivia turned the tap and began splashing water onto her face and hands. "We were told not to get more than the allowed amount. But everyone ignored that." Cupping her hands, she lapped the water into her mouth.

"How would they know?" Cristal asked.

Her mom shook her head, wiping her lips with her hand.

"They monitor us with this chip." Lifting her arm, she pulled down her sleeve to reveal a pink scar.

"And did GN do anything about it?"

"Yes, GN fixed the problem by making the sensors release water with thirty second interval breaks while the guards made sure the line up moved at a steady pace. The showers have auto sensors too. One-minute showers. Otherwise it's a wet wash cloth," her mother said, glancing around the room.

"So where are we exactly?"

Raffe met Olivia's gaze with a cool stare. She returned his stare with a challenge of her own. When mom wanted answers, there was no way around it. The awkward staring battle lasted for half a minute until Raffe turned to the stove.

"Megiddo," he said, scooping food onto a plate.

"Ah," Olivia said, smiling to herself, pleased to get her answer. "Is Megiddo a special place?"

Cristal's patience was wearing thin. There was only so

much chitchat she could tolerate in one day. She pushed the chair back and got to her feet.

Raffe pointed the spatula in her direction. "Where do you think you're going?"

Her fingers clenched into a fist. *Let it go, Cristal.*

"What are we doing? Playing twenty questions? Shouldn't we be out there trying to fight demons and save the world?"

He scooped a spoonful of *shakshouka* onto another plate.

"Patience. Consider this a short moment of calm before the storm," he said.

He slid the plate to her. "Eat. You will need all the energy for what is to come."

"What is to come?" her mother asked as she seated herself at the table.

She was about to reply when her bracelet began vibrating in short pulses. She glanced up to see her mother and Raffe deeply engrossed in conversation.

Time to find out who was trying to contact her.

"This is heavenly," she could hear her mother say. "You obviously enjoy cooking."

Oh brother.

"Something wrong, Cristal?" Raffe asked. "You have not touched your food." He seated himself directly across from her, eying her plate.

"Waiting for it to cool down," she said.

Need to get him off my back.

She grabbed the fork and took a bite. Surprisingly, the flavors of cinnamon, cumin and allspice melded perfectly with the sweet taste of the tomatoes and the yolks of the eggs. Whoever was contacting her would have to wait.

"You must be starving," he said.

85

"I got used to eating the sludge at GN. I have to admit, your cooking is very good," she finally said after wolfing down half her plate.

"Divine is what you mean to say," he replied, placing his fork down. "Angels think hunger is a human weakness. Only after I first transformed into human form did I comprehend the pleasure of eating."

Olivia looked up at him, her eyes softening. "God gave us such special gifts. We humans always take them for granted."

Ugh. Just like mom to get all religious again.

The bracelet shook in persistent pulses. No one else noticed confirming its invisibility.

Cristal polished off the rest of the meal.

"Delish," she said, licking her lips and patting her stomach. She knew he enjoyed impressing her with his human talents.

As predicted, Raffe's smile stretched from ear to ear.

"Want seconds?" he asked.

She grabbed her plate. "No thanks, I'm stuffed," she said, making her way to the sink.

"Are you certain? There is more in the pan."

Cristal turned the tap. "Really, I'm full. If I had space, trust me, I'd be eating a whole lot more."

Raffe chuckled and said, "Olivia, you need to learn how to make this for your daughter."

The distraction was perfect timing. Raffe began explaining to Olivia the art of cooking *shakshouka*.

In the stream of water a white rectangle materialized. Inside the rectangle was Gabriel with his crooked nose, dreadlocks and all.

She began blinking in Morse code.

... .. --. -.

S-I-G-N

The code meant it wasn't safe to talk.

He gave a quick nod and began communicating in sign language.

She caught her breath.

The message said: *Get out now.*

CHAPTER 16
WHERE ANGELS FEAR

Kerim hung his jacket on the hook and shut the locker door. There were rumors that those in the resistance were preparing to join other resistance groups. Without Harry, the people were becoming restless.

His earpiece beeped.

"The hobbit is en route. He just entered the elevator," Joanna Chan's voice said in his ear.

Joanna was one of Harry's top Truth Seekers and Kerim was glad to have her as his eyes and ears.

What did Lionheart's right-hand minion want now?

Before he could answer his question, George Beaver threw open the change room door.

"Beaver, didn't I tell you that hobbits aren't allowed on this floor?"

The greasy faced imp crossed his arms and puffed out his chest. "Remember who you're speaking with. I could have you fired in a snap."

Kerim gave him a smirk. "So Lionheart sent Santa's helper to give me that message."

"Hardy har har," Beaver replied, pushing his black-rimmed glasses up his pug nose. He marched up to Kerim and stuck his finger in his face. "You better watch it buddy."

Kerim grabbed it and gave it a sharp twist.

"Owww! Hey, stop it!" Beaver cried.

Kerim tightened his grip and leaned over. "Point that thing at me again," he said in a low voice, "and you'll only be counting to four with this hand."

"Okay, okay," Beaver said, trying to pull away. "I promise I won't do it again."

"Get out of my way." Kerim shoved the annoying man into the locker and slammed it shut. It was something he wanted to do months ago.

"Hey! You're not going to get away with this!" Beaver called out, banging the door.

Kerim heaved a sigh. He walked down the hall straight to the supply closet. He tapped his earpiece and said, "Do you have eyes on Lionheart's office?"

"Rupert's on duty and outside her door," Joanna said.

Rupert was one of his human resistance fighters. Lionheart's entourage was usually of the demon kind. Something was up.

"When did he take on the shift?" he asked, stepping into the closet and closing the door behind him.

"Just a sec, I'm scrubbing through the video now," she said. "Okay, ten minutes ago. Looks like Lionheart's guard ordered him to take his shift a few minutes before that."

He stood in the darkness.

Bezel's presence on Earth put the world in constant

upheaval. In the past year floods, hurricanes, earthquakes and other disasters were pummelling former first world countries. Food and water shortages were now considered the norm. GN's RFID chip program was introduced to help ration supplies and coordinate housing for the masses.

Those who were chipped were now easy to track. Those who had refused the chip now suffered hunger and persecution.

Those in power, a handful of humans, angels and demons, became more powerful.

Everyone had his bloody agenda. Wading through the crap wasn't getting any easier.

Another beep in his ear.

"What is it?" he said sharply.

"Jenna just confirmed that senior managers are heading to the conference room for a mandatory meeting," Joanna said. He could hear her fingers tapping on her keyboard.

Something was happening. This was the first time he wasn't in the know.

"I'm on my way," he said, tapping the earpiece off.

No time to walk across campus.

He waved his hand. The atoms from the back wall dispersed and he stepped into it.

Suspended in space for a brief moment, he contemplated changing course altogether and head to Tel Aviv.

"All in good time," he told himself.

Metal walls materialized around him. The bottom of his boots smacked against tile.

There was a faint sound of water, then footsteps and the creaking of the door swinging open and closing shut.

He pulled open the door and stepped out of the stall. No humans in the vicinity.

He walked over to the sink and stared at his human reflection. Dark shadows under his eyes and deep lines creased his forehead. He should take better care of his human form.

He placed his hands under the tap. Out came a short burst of water. He could have commanded for more. If humans had to sacrifice, he was resigned to do so too.

His senses picked up a supernatural force in close range.

He brushed his hands on his jeans.

Time to get going.

CHAPTER 17
LIONHEART

Lionheart materialized before him enveloped in a black dress that clung to the curves of her human form.

Parting her robust red lips in a provocative half-smile, she asked, "What is so urgent that you had to take me away from my duties?"

He narrowed his eyes. "You're holding secret meetings?"

She crossed her arms over her full bosom. "Are you jealous you're not invited?"

"Stop playing with me," he said.

The smile faded from her face. "As you are aware, there have been a number of human staff who have gone missing. I called all the senior managers to the conference room to get some answers."

"Your demon crew have gone AWOL. Or are they in a meeting too?" he asked.

Her face grew dark. "AWOL? I noticed that Wenthall

wasn't posted outside my office. I thought you had arranged this."

He shook his head. "The spikes of spiritual activity correlate with the latest events around the White House."

"Are you saying that my demons had something to do with the kidnapping of President Roshenabaum?"

"Do you have evidence that proves otherwise?"

The surrounding energy thickened and the concrete walls heaved in and out.

"Looks like we have company," he said quietly.

Her eyes widened. She glanced over her shoulder. "What is happening?"

"I was going to ask you the same thing," he said.

Suddenly, the door erupted into flames turning the walls a bright orange.

Kerim grabbed Lionheart by the arm.

GN soldiers stepped into the room. Standing in the front of the pack was Lionheart's personal soldier.

She pulled away from Kerim's grip.

"Wenthall, what the hell is going on here?" she snapped.

The soldier's face contorted as he spoke—the bones in his jaw twisting and stretching.

"We've watched the disasters destroy everything. Humans are disappearing in the thousands and the RFID chips can't trace them. You told us that you'd get Bezel's ear, but it seems he's obsessed with charming humans to believe he's the new savior. His presence has stifled our ability to travel outside this decrepit country yet you do nothing to stop him."

Green scales ripped through his skin. The pupils in his eyes compressed into vertical slits while a forked tongue slid in and out of his gaping jaws.

She said in a quiet tone. "And what exactly, pray tell, do you expect me to do to stop him?"

"You're no leader," he hissed. "We're not the only ones who think so."

"Is that so? So you think you and your low level demon friends can stand up to me?"

As she spoke, her statuesque body began doubling in size. Slate colored metallic feathers with razor-sharp tips ruptured through her back producing wings of malleable steel.

"Go back from whence you came," she said in a booming voice. A lightning bolt shot down from the ceiling and tore the demon in half. Wentall didn't have a chance.

She pointed her talon-like finger at the others.

"Who's next?"

The soldiers cowered and moved backwards en masse exposing one who was a foot shorter than all of them and probably weighed less than a sack of cement.

Lionheart put her hands on her hips. "Bow before me lowly demon lest I unleash my wrath on you."

The insignificant soldier gave her a blank stare.

"Either he was as stupid as he looked or..." Kerim thought.

In an unexpected turn of events, the soldier transformed into a pillar of black smoke.

A magnetic sound began reverberating around the room shattering the mirrors and cracking the wall and floor tile.

"You, Lionheart will bow before me along with your angel friend," said the entity before them.

Kerim couldn't determine the demon's identity. He couldn't determine if this thing was even a demon.

The black smoke rose and swirled in and around the soldiers, creeping into their orifices. They opened their mouths as if to protest, but the smoke silenced their screams. One by one, they shrivelled into piles of ashes.

"Now time to rid this world of your filth," the spiritual being said.

Lionheart put her hands together and shot a blast of fiery energy.

"Not so fast. Identify yourself," she said moving forward.

"No, don't!" Kerim cried out.

Lionheart's eyes widened. The curls of smoke brushed against her, melting the feathers off her back. The pain ran through her in violent waves. The realization that this was not any ordinary demon before her was reflected in the stunned expression on her face.

The black smoke was taking shape. "Archangel, I could use someone like you." The entity moved towards them. "But first, I must snuff out your lady friend."

The dark entity rushed towards Lionheart.

Kerim had little choice but to pull her close. "If you tell anyone about this, I'll deny it," he said.

She nodded.

High pitched howls flooded the air and the ground shuddered beneath their feet.

"Hold on," he said, holding her against him. The energy surged from inside him.

The human emotions were exhausting to control. But tame them he must.

The next part of the mission was now in motion. There was no going back.

CHAPTER 18
LIMBO

C ristal twisted and untwisted a strand of hair that hung over her eye. How to get out of the safe house without raising Raffe's suspicions? Facing his wrath wasn't something she was prepared to do just yet.

She endured listening to Raffe and her mother chatter away about angels and demons as if they were discussing the top ten apocalyptic films of the year.

What if she left Olivia behind?

Deep down in her gut though, she knew she couldn't. She was her mother after all.

As time passed, Gabriel's dire warning lost its urgency. She held back a yawn. *Can't keep my eyes open.*

Finally Raffe stood up. "It's late."

"Yes, it's time for bed," Cristal said, wondering why Gabriel had sent her the dire warning. Throughout the whole evening, there had been no signs of imminent danger or threat.

Olivia gave a tired smile. "Yes, it has been a long day."

He replied, "Stay here in this room. Just a reminder that our lovely hosts are fast asleep. Please do not go beyond here and the kitchen or risk waking them."

"And where will you sleep? Unless angels don't sleep?" her mother asked.

"I have some business to do upstairs," he said, his thumb motioning upward.

"Are there rooms upstairs?" Olivia asked.

Cristal sighed. "Mom, he's talking about the other Upstairs."

"Ah, right, of course."

Raffe chuckled. "Very good then. I will be back before the family awakens."

"And what will we be doing tomorrow?" Cristal asked.

"There are things to be done in town. Then we journey to find someone," Raffe said.

"Who?" her mother asked.

"No more questions," he said, turning towards the hallway. "I have much to do before the sun rises."

And with that, they were dismissed.

She half expected him to transform into an angel and fly off in dramatic fashion. It would have impressed her mother to pieces. Instead, he walked with brisk steps into the kitchen and slipped out the back door.

Olivia stood staring after him.

"Mom, he's gone. Let's get some rest."

The sofa seemed to be calling for her. She knew that she'd have to settle for the chair.

"Mom, you can take the couch," she said. "I need to crash for a few minutes." And reboot.

A crochet blanket lay on the couch. Walid's mother had spent many evenings crocheting the intricate pattern. Cristal felt a twinge in her heart. The closeness she felt when she was with *Im Walid* was difficult to describe. She was the mother she never had. And now the strangeness of being here in her home with her real mother was beyond surreal.

She heaved a sigh.

"Here, you can have the blanket," she said, turning to her. Her eyes widened when she realized that her mom had left the room.

"Mom?"

She threw the blanket on the couch and ran out.

"Mom!"

The hall was darker and denser than she recalled it ever being. It reminded her of the back of the closet. A shiver ran down her spine.

"Where are you?" she called out, her voice shaking.

A door creaked open, then shuffling sounds, followed by her mom's voice.

"Just want to go for a little tour," her mom said.

What would Walid's mother think of having them in her house uninvited and at this late hour?

"Raffe said not to bother anyone," Cristal said in a loud whisper.

She stumbled forward, straining to see through the black velvet curtain of darkness. The hallway seemed longer than she remembered. Thoughts were darting around in her head. Something just wasn't right. Her heart thudded in staccato against her ribcage.

"Mom! Come back here," she said, only knowing that calling out for her was pointless.

Soft voices caught her attention. She continued into the darkness, reaching out her hands.

"You must hurry," a woman said.

Her mother's voice pierced through the air. "I thought you were dead!"

Cristal rushed towards the sound. To her right, a doorway took shape. The voices were coming from the other side.

"Mom, are you okay?" she called out.

"We are in grave danger," the woman said. "We must go now."

Cristal stepped into the doorway. Her foot landed on a spongy surface. A gray fog surrounded her.

"Mom, where are you?"

Someone with strong fingers grabbed her by the elbow in a forceful but gentle manner.

"Keep your voice down," the man said in a hushed whisper.

She yanked her arm back. "Reveal yourself," she commanded.

The fog melted from the ground upwards. The form of the man became visible. Tall, with shoulders that once were broad but now softened by age. The outline of the face was wide with wavy dark hair framing it. The eyes grabbed her attention. Dark charcoal brown, set deep under his brow. Tiny crow's feet lined the corners when his face relaxed into a smile.

"Dad," she said softly.

He pulled her into his arms burying her face into his chest which heaved in waves of sobs.

"Cristal, my sweet child," he said into her hair.

She clung to him. "Dad, I missed you so much."

"We must go now," the woman said.

Cristal glanced up to see another familiar face. She had seen it in the sky the day the first earthquake took place. The woman's face had been painted with angry red strokes in the sky.

"Mrs. Doub?" she asked.

The woman gave her a gentle smile, her brown eyes softening. "Yes, my child. I am Harry's mother, but my name is Bina Schwartz. Never took my husband's name. I was a liberal feminist even then." She chuckled to herself softly.

To her right, stood her own mother Olivia, whose eyes were wide with disbelief and confusion.

"Carlos, did you run away with this woman?" she cried out, reaching for him like a jealous wife. "You left me for...her?"

He reached out to Olivia, holding her shoulder firmly. "We don't have time to explain. Raffe will be returning soon and we must leave now."

Olivia shook her head in anger. "What does Raffe have to do with all this? You left me with a young daughter to raise by myself. And now you think you can talk your way out of it?"

Her father glanced away before replying.

"My dear Olivia," he said. "If you loved me for even a fraction of our time together, listen to me. We need to leave now."

"Hurry. He has returned!" Bina called out, raising her hand.

Cristal moved towards her. "Let me help," she said.

Bina reached out. "Come, dear."

They joined hands.

Carlos motioned for Olivia to come.

"I'm staying." She folded her arms on her chest.

A thunderous roar suddenly filled their ears.

"Now!" Bina said, grasping her hand.

Cristal shuddered as the energy surged from inside her and out through her fingers.

A bright pillar of light shot from beneath their feet to the sky.

Olivia's jaw dropped, her gaze drawn to the light. "Cristal, what's happening to you?"

Carlos waved to her. "Come with us!"

Olivia took a step forward. "Where are you going?"

In the doorframe behind her, something moved. She turned toward the noise.

"Mom!" Cristal cried. "Run!"

Olivia moved towards them, a look of uncertainty crossing her face.

Inside the doorway, Raffe stepped forward transformed in his full angel glory, wings spread behind him.

He smiled just then—a very unnerving smile.

CHAPTER 19
CHANGE OF PLANS

Harry's patience was running out. They had spent hours mapping out a plan to break into GN Tel Aviv.

"Who knows where that closet will take us?" Serena asked.

"Closet?" Walid asked. "We break into GN to get to a closet?"

Harry had to admit it was a half-baked plan.

They were hunched over the laptop when he caught something flickering.

"Did you see that?" Walid whispered.

Serena chimed in. "Yeah, looks like we have a guest."

Harry tensed his fists, ready to call upon his powers.

"In the name of God Almighty, reveal yourself!" he commanded.

A shadowy figure in the shape of a man began materializing. The wiry build and the pile of dreadlocks crowning his head confirmed that it was none other than Gabriel.

Walid leapt up from the chair. "I got him," he cried out. He slid across the table and charged towards him.

"Hold up," Harry called out.

Walid ran through Gabriel's body and out the other side, careening into the concrete wall. He stumbled back, rubbing his shoulder and shaking his head in confusion.

Serena struggled to hold back her laughter.

"Stand down, soldier. Gabriel is one of us."

Still rubbing his shoulder, he turned to them. "Gabriel? The same Gabriel you say died on day of the earthquake?"

Gabriel lifted his chin in acknowledgement. "The one and only."

Walid gave a bewildered look. "But I can see you with my own eyes."

Serena patted his shoulder. "It's because you see dead people."

A mixture of fear and curiosity crossed his face.

She looked back at Gabriel. "So why can't you enter a room like a normal person instead of scaring our poor friend here?"

"I can materialize in solid form but need to keep my energy for later," he said in an unusually somber tone. "Good to see all of you, but we don't have much time."

The seriousness in his tone instantly sobered everyone's mood.

"Debrief us then," Harry said, leaning back against the table.

"Cristal is in Megiddo," Gabriel said.

Serena glanced over at Harry. "She's here?"

A dark shadow crossed Gabriel's face. "No. She's in the other Megiddo."

"Other Megiddo?" she asked. "What does that mean?"

Harry felt his stomach sink. He had hoped it wouldn't come to this.

Just then the room swayed beneath their feet and the walls swelled in and out in subtle waves.

"Let go of me!" Serena cried out.

"Something is holding me!" Walid struggled to move his arms.

"Gabriel!" Harry called out. "Tell whoever you're working with to release them immediately."

Gabriel glided towards the wall, his lips moving like he was having a silent conversation with an unseen person.

A small indent in the center of the wall began expanding and tearing up the plaster and opening a black hole—a portal to the "other side."

Harry called out again. "Whoever you are, I command you in the name of Almighty God to release my friends immediately."

The invisible force complied and released its stronghold on Serena and Walid.

Walid leaned forward putting his hands on his knees. His lungs burned as he tried to take a breath. "What is going on?"

Serena moved into a defensive stance. "You believe in angels and demons, right?"

He tried to keep a brave face. "*Akeed*. Of course."

Harry stepped in between them. "This is not your fight, Walid. You have a family to protect."

"No," he replied. "I am Truth Seeker now. I go where you go."

Serena interrupted. "Harry is right. We can't promise your safety."

Walid took a deep breath and looked up at him. Whether it was bravery or blind faith, Walid's decision was made. They bumped fists forming a silent pact.

The marble tile shifted beneath their feet. Walid's look of determination wavered for a moment. What followed was an ear-piercing screech that made the fillings in his teeth rattle.

Gabriel waved to them. "Come on! The portal is closing."

Without missing a beat, Serena had already made it over to the portal. She glanced back at Harry, her brows furrowed. He'd seen that look many times before.

"What are you waiting for?" she called out.

What could he say? Something felt off about the whole thing. Yes, Gabriel was their friend, but treading cautiously was how he always played it in online games and also in the real world. Serena was a dare-devil. A risk taker. He admired that. But still, that nagging gut feeling was telling him that they needed to slow down and rethink their next move.

He lifted his hand to signal her to stop, but his hesitation only made Serena more determined.

A look of disappointment swept across her face. Without her usual arguing, she stepped into the portal opening and disappeared.

"Serena! Don't go!"

He turned to Walid whose eyes were wide with uncertainty.

"Are you ready for this?" he asked.

He nodded, but his expression said otherwise.

"Sorry to break up this touching moment," Gabriel said. "I'll see you both on the other side." And with that, he too disappeared into the portal.

Walid marched over to the opening. "We must go now," he

said firmly. He closed his eyes, his lips moving silently in prayer. When his eyes opened, he gave Harry a nod and stepped into the opening disappearing into the hole.

What kind of leader would he be to let his Truth Seekers cross over without him? Harry had to make a decision.

Against his own instincts, he followed Walid through the portal into the dark unknown.

CHAPTER 20
OTHER MEGIDDO

Raffe standing before them in his full angel glory was a wondrous and terrifying sight. Cristal saw a look of wonder and fear cross her father's face.

Raffe stepped forward, the heel of his golden boot scuffing the tile. "A family reunion," he said, drawing out his words. "I have finally captured the two most elusive pair of souls."

Her dad gasped, his hand clutching his chest. "Don't respond. We need to get out now."

He was right. Responding to Raffe would only slow them down. Instead she began reciting the Lord's Prayer.

"Our Father who art in Heaven..."

Raffe crossed his arms. "I'm simply the messenger, not your enemy. You need not fear me."

"Fear you?" she cried. "Don't be mistaken."

He shook his head. "My child, as I said, I'm only a messenger of God. Your mission is to bring ..."

There he was trying to trick her again. She summoned her inner powers.

"Dear God, please bring us..." she began.

"To kingdom come," Raffe interrupted.

Ignore him. "Take us, oh Lord, safely away from here."

The smile on Raffe's face twisted into a scowl while a brilliant flash of light blasted around them.

❦

Moments later they landed in the only place she could think of to go—her safe place.

The plucking of harp strings filled her ears and a gentle breeze welcomed them. The familiar mist that covered the fields of soft golden grass reached out and caressed her skin.

"Where are we?" her dad asked, still clutching his chest.

Her heart raced while her insides shook. Teleporting so many people wasn't as easy as she thought.

"It's okay. We're safe for now," she managed to say.

He spun around. "Is everyone okay?"

"I'm here." Bina said as she struggled to stand.

Cristal did a quick scan to find her mother sprawled face first on the ground. She scrambled to her side. Her dad did the same.

"Mom!"

"Olivia, can you hear us?"

Bina cried out. "We need to get her back to the other side. Her human body is not meant for this world."

"So she's not..." Cristal started to say.

"...dead like me?"

He had finished her thought. Death was another phase of the journey, but the reality was hard to grasp.

He lifted Olivia into his arms. "Cristal, you must hurry and get her out of here."

He was right. There was no time to waste. With that, she threw her arms up. "I'll take us all back to the world of the living."

"No!" Bina appeared before her, panic bulging from her eyes. "We cannot go back. Carlos and I'll be trapped in our comatose bodies. Take care of your mother. I'll take your father to Limbo."

What was she talking about? "But I just got you both out of there."

"Don't worry," her dad said. "We'll be fine."

"But, dad."

"Take your mom to the land of the living. Be strong. Just like I taught you."

She buried her head into his shoulder seeking the comfort of his arms. The soft glow of heavenly light created an aura around them.

"Take her now before it's too late," he said gently pulling away.

The child in her refused to listen.

"What if we just stay here?" she asked, imagining how her foot would've stamped the ground years ago.

Trumpets blaring from above abruptly ended the discussion.

Bina's eyes widened. "Have you heard this sound here before?"

Cristal shook her head. "No. It's usually very peaceful here."

The mist that caressed and eased her uncertainties was now transforming into a dense fog.

"This isn't a coincidence! You must leave now!" Bina cried.

Taking her cue, she drew upon her powers and called out, "Dear God, please help us all."

A loud crack of thunder clapped and was followed by a loud wind that howled around them. Instinctively, Cristal reached out and grabbed her mother's hand.

"We will contact you again!" her dad said as Bina touched the ground. They both vanished a second before a wave of energy grabbed hold of her.

"Hold on, mom," she said under her breath as the rushing wind threw them headlong into the place between the spiritual and earthly worlds.

CHAPTER 21
JELLYFISH

Lionheart placed her arm across the back of the couch, letting her long red nail scrape the dark leather grain. She allowed herself the pleasure of burying her feet into the softness of the white shag carpet.

"Is this a safe house?" Lionheart asked.

Kerim was busy peering in the fridge. "This place is frozen in time. They can't find us here." He grabbed a bottle of beer from the door and twisted off the cap.

"Good," she said.

He grabbed another and walked over to her.

"Here, this might take the edge off," he said, handing her the bottle. He eased himself into the chair and put his boots on the coffee table. He gave a small smirk, remembering Cristal scolding him for his bad manners.

Lionheart twisted off the cap and took a sip. "Haven't had one of these in decades."

"You don't know what you're missing," he said chugging down the rest.

It felt good to take a break. The warmness in his gut and the slight buzz was just what he needed. Hopefully Lionheart would unwind a bit before they began their strategic planning.

She shifted in her seat, glancing over her shoulder from time-to-time.

"Relax. We're safe. That's why this is called a safe house," he said, running his hand through his hair.

Under her down turned brow, her eyes narrowed into angry slits, the irises around her pupils lighting up like burning amber.

"Safe? You broke the rules when you let Harry and Serena cross over to Tel Aviv. And for what? To free that girl who started all of this? I want to know how were they able to cross over? Did you help them? Even I can't transport myself outside of the country since Bezel was let loose on Earth."

He didn't need or want to be lectured especially when he was struggling to silence the ghastly pulsing in his temples.

She continued. "The only thing that's keeping me from obliterating you is the sliver of hope that this girl is the one who can save us."

The awful migraine pummeled the inside of his cranium. He put his hands over his ears—a human reaction.

"Kerim? Are you listening to me?" she hissed.

Oddly, her voice was fading, sounding more distant and muffled with each pounding throb.

Suddenly flashes of the present and the past raced through his mind. He found himself slipping away from the mortal plane, almost like he was about to transport through to the spiritual realm.

"Are you okay? Kerim, you're scaring me."

Cristal's voice was in his ear and yet his human brain fought to believe it.

He managed to open his eyes to see Lionheart's face looming over his. She was trying to talk to him, but the constant pounding drowned out her words. He tried to read her lips.

She was saying, "don't dare take off without me."

He wasn't surprised she could be so self-serving.

The oxygen, which his human lungs depended upon, burned his throat while a howling wind whipped circles around him.

Out of the corner of his eye, a jelly-like entity the size of a fridge manifested itself. The thing slammed into him, its tentacle-like appendages wrapping around his body. Except for his face, the jelly crap covered every inch of his body. He tried to free himself. The more he struggled, the tighter the blob squeezed. Transforming was an exhaustive process for even a seasoned archangel. What was second nature for him was proving to be impossible. The bloody "thing" was draining him of his supernatural powers.

He'd been in battles against the most formidable of demons. Blasting this giant jellyfish should be child's play.

He directed his powers outward. The thing squeezed back with equal force. He heard a loud snap followed by throbbing waves up his legs. Fire burned into his bones.

A voice, or what resembled one, entered his head. "Relax."

Surrendering wasn't his MO, *modus operandi*. He clenched his fist sending more pain through his arms.

"Relax," it said again.

"Who are you? Reveal your identity," he commanded.

Another voice, a familiar one said, "Are you sure you know what you're doing?"

The first voice replied, "This is only the second time I've done this. It's not like the first time. Kidnapping an angel isn't the same as a human."

What was going on? First, a jellyfish attacks him and now he was hearing voices?

"We need to bring him here," the first voice continued. "He is the only one powerful enough to stand up to another archangel."

Suddenly it all made sense. The unconventional spiritual attack on him had the earmarks of one who was neither a demon nor an angel. What spiritual being in their right mind would dare kidnap an angel of his ranking?

The first voice was masked by some kind of filter, but he knew it could only belong to one person.

CHAPTER 22
HULDA

The winds had died down to a dull hum. Lionheart was pacing back and forth. Things had taken an unusual turn. Kerim had to make the best of the situation.

"Is this what an enchilada feels like?" he mumbled.

"Always joking around. We need to find out who the hell is after us!" Lionheart cried.

"What do you mean 'us'?"

She switched gears. "You look awful. Maybe I can peel this stuff off," she said, reaching out to him.

"Don't," he said. "This junk will latch on you too."

She sat back on her heels. "Can't you leave your mortal body. Change back to your real form?"

"Wow, why I didn't think of that first?"

Lionheart rose to her feet and moved away.

"Hey," he said, "where are you going?"

She turned, tears streaking her cheeks. The warrior he knew her to be was a human emotional mess.

"You're wrecking that black junk on your eyes," he said, softening his tone.

She swiped her cheeks with the back of her hand. "It's mascara, you imbecile," she mumbled.

The jelly cocoon tightened around him.

"Here we go again," he said. *Have to stop struggling.* He breathed in as much as he could, then out, the pain slicing his lungs.

"What happened to us?" she asked. "How did we end up in this mess?"

It was just like Lionheart to be oblivious of his physical agony. She probably hadn't felt mortal physical pain for centuries. When angels transformed in human form for the first time, they were intrigued with being completely human. They wanted it all—emotions, senses and all.

It wasn't long before the novelty wore out. Most resorted to only enabling the human emotions and blocking out physical pain. An epidural of the senses, Lionheart used to say.

Strange thoughts entered his head. The world they knew was coming to an end. Was this it? His impending death?

The closest thing to death an angel could encounter was an eternity of suspension, a coma-like darkness, disconnected forever from the spiritual and mortal worlds. Most angels feared this place. But after eons of battling, death was looking like a good state to be in.

A sharp smack stung his cheek.

"Oh no you don't. You're not going to leave me that easy," Lionheart said, her voice shaking the floor beneath him.

He forced his eyes open, bracing for another slap. But instead of seeing her open palm, Lionheart was on the ground on her knees with her hands clasped together in fervent prayer.

"Dear Almighty God," she was saying. "I know I am not worthy of Your attention. I have sinned beyond forgiving. I pray now not for myself but for Your servant Kerim."

A deep sadness tore through him. Just seeing Lionheart praying and allowing herself to be submissive on his behalf made his heart ache.

When she fell to Earth centuries ago. Only then, she wasn't a "she," at least in the mortal sense. Serving alongside him, an angel in the Almighty's army, Lionheart was genderless, as God had created all angels: spiritual and immortal, with no ability to reproduce.

During their arduous training, they were taught how to take a physical form. Most angels chose the male human form. It was the obvious choice. They wanted to be like God's first mortal creation.

However, a small group of angels transformed themselves into female form.

"I always wondered why you chose the female form," he said, but it sounded more like a gasp for air.

Angels never questioned each other's choice. It was an unspoken sign of respect. In his human state, with his powers diminishing and his physical body being crushed to a pulp, Kerim's curiosity needed to be satisfied.

Lionheart looked up from her hands, locking her gaze with his.

Her eyes like amber liquid burned through him. The caramel color of her skin, the strong cheekbones overtop the fullness of her lips still captivated him. Even in her broken state, she was magnificent.

He struggled to speak. "Tell me, why female?"

"What are you talking about?" she asked looking away. "That was a long long time ago."

He tried to speak, but the words sat like quicksand in his head.

Mumble. Grunt. Say something.

Not being able to speak was incredibly unsettling.

After a moment of silence, she turned to him.

"I choose not to think about those days," she said. "You sure you want to hear it?"

His silence served as a yes.

Lionheart gave a dramatic sigh and opened her arms delicately like a ballerina.

"The Almighty gave me my first assignment," she paused, closing her eyes to envision the memory. "Yes, I remember it well. I was asked to watch over a young girl named Hulda. You knew I wasn't thrilled with this. Why not a king, I asked you? Or a leader? Why had God given me such an insignificant assignment?

"We weren't allowed to question Him. I resigned myself to do my duty as best as I could. Hulda's early years were uneventful. She was a good child and devoted to serving the Almighty. I came to understand through the child's eyes how mortals saw each other and the world around them. To her, the world was a very small place. Despite this narrow vision of her existence, the child's love for the Almighty was fascinating.

"Later during the reign of Josiah, the king sought for Hulda to help him interpret a message from God. He believed that a woman's compassion would not twist the meaning. It amazed me how a powerful king sought the guidance from a female adviser instead of all the male advisers who served him."

Lionheart turned to him. "It was then I chose to take the female form."

His lips parted searching for words that fell off his tongue before he could form them.

"Kerim, stay with me."

He closed his eyes, imagining that his physical body was fusing together with the entity around him. Who knew that a mortal would be the cause of his demise?

"Let me see if I can remove that vile shroud once and for all."

A flood of heat surrounded him. He could hear Lionheart calling him, but the sound was fading further and further into the distance. Stuck in mortal form meant he would die a mortal death. Even Lionheart couldn't stop this.

Only God could save him now.

PART III
THY KINGDOM COME

Reveal

Thy Will be done
on Earth as it is in Heaven

CHAPTER 23
CULPRITS

Harry couldn't believe it had come to this. He'd been standing with his arms in the air; sweat pouring from his brow, and white light blasting from his chest for the past half hour.

"Harry! Stop it! You're killing him!" Serena yelled.

"I won't have enough energy to try later," he said under his breath.

"What good would it do us if he's dead?"

"Angels can't die," he said through gritted teeth.

"What if that isn't true?"

Her words hung in the air like a sinister warning. Floating above them was a virtual screen filled with the image of Kerim wrapped in the spiritual cytoplasm that Harry had inadvertently encased him with.

"I wish we could hear what they're saying," he mumbled.

"The apartment is a safe house. Technically, we shouldn't even be getting a visual feed," Gabriel said.

Serena paced back and forth. "You don't need audio to see that he's dying! Look at Lionheart! She's on her knees praying, for God's sake!"

"You said that Harry successfully teleported another person before this. Right?" Walid asked.

Serena mumbled. "That was only during spiritual training."

He frowned. "Then we must have faith that he will succeed again. A wife needs to help her husband and not doubt him."

She crossed her arms over her chest. "The guy teleported over but left behind parts in the process."

"Parts?" Walid turned to Harry.

Harry didn't know what was crazier, trying to teleport an archangel or listening to this insane conversation.

The blast of white light that was rushing through him was losing its intensity. Concentrate. He had to get Kerim over to this side. A lot of souls depended on it.

His mother's voice entered his head. "Careful, Harry. You don't want to kill him. Without him, the end of humanity is inevitable."

Harry couldn't believe his ears. "You told us to bring him over and that's what I'm trying to do here."

A deeper voice interrupted. "You could have tried to persuade him to come over instead of wrapping him up like a ridiculous burrito," Carlos said.

The idea that negotiating with Kerim would have been a better plan was absurd. Kerim would never have gone for it.

Serena interrupted the conversation in his head. "This shouldn't be happening."

There were too many questions. The ground was heaving

beneath his feet. He blinked hard. Everything was spinning around him.

"Harry!" Serena screamed.

The energy blast lost its steam. He keeled forward, his head smacking the floor. The teleportation attempt had officially failed.

⚜

HARRY AWOKE TO FIND HIMSELF ALONE ON THE COUCH. HE could hear voices in the other room. Walid's kitchen had become a makeshift headquarters. From the hushed conversation, plans were being made without him.

His head was foggy recollecting the moments that brought them here. When they had crossed over from the bakery, he had blindly thought they'd be landing in the "other" Megiddo to save Cristal. Instead they landed in a cemented yard.

Walid had rushed over to him. "This is my house!"

"Your house?" he asked. "What's going on?"

He could hear Serena's voice. He glanced up and saw her at the top of the stairs.

"Come," Walid said, waving his hand. "My mother said to come inside right away."

Harry followed him up the stairs and stopped behind Serena who was surrounded by three young girls who stared at him, their moon shaped eyes so much like Walid's.

Serena turned to him, her expression filled with anxiety. "Walid's sisters say that Cristal isn't here."

He pulled her into an embrace. "Are you okay?"

"What's going on? Why did we teleport across town?"

In Arabic, Walid spoke sternly to his sisters. *"Foot joo-ah.* Go inside now."

The three girls nodded and slipped inside the doorway.

"Where's Gabriel?" Harry asked.

Walid shrugged. "I have not seen him."

Just then, a cold breeze swept around them in circles. Serena's tiny frame shivered against him.

"He's here," she said.

Another gust of frigid air whirled around them. If Gabriel was trying to scare them, he was doing a crappy job at it.

"Enough! Gabriel, reveal yourself!" he snapped.

A voice entered his head. "This place is close to the portal to Limbo. I can't transform into physical form here."

Serena's voice entered the conversation. "You tricked us."

"No, I didn't."

"Then you've got some explaining to do."

Harry was about to add a more colorful comment when someone stepped into the doorway.

A man dressed in a traditional Arabic two-piece thobe, a long cotton sleeved shirt that flowed down to his knees over loose pants of the same material, opened his arms.

The man standing before him with the disheveled comb-over and beak-like nose needed no introductions.

"Harrell," the man said in his deep gravelly way.

"Dad."

"Look at you! You are not a little boy anymore."

With one of his wide palmed hands, Aaron gave him three hearty smacks on the back. His dad's awkwardness was punctuated with odd signs of what only Harry could interpret as affection.

"Okay, don't get all fatherly on me. Tell me why we're here."

Aaron gave him a small smile. "Aren't you going to introduce me to my daughter-in-law?"

Serena reached out her hand, the smile on her face stretching from ear to ear. "Happy to finally meet you, Mr. Doub."

"No need for that. We're family now. Call me Dad." And with that, Harry watched dumbfounded as his dad reached out and gave her a bear hug.

"Dad," she said, her voice muffled in his chest.

When they pulled apart, it was hard not to notice the loving look on his father's face. Ridiculous as it seemed, Harry felt a twinge of jealousy.

"Now let's go inside and answer the questions I can see swirling in your heads," his dad said in his big professor voice, bellowing out the words as if he were standing in a five hundred-seat lecture hall.

He turned on one heel wobbling slightly before managing to balance himself.

"He's so sweet," Serena said.

This clumsiness was what his followers found endearing. For Harry, it was as annoying now as it was when he was a kid.

"See you all on the inside," Aaron Doub called out before stepping through the doorway.

Verdict reached. His dad was still the biggest nerd in the world.

CHAPTER 24
CHAOS

When she thought she had finally mastered the art of teleporting, Cristal now found herself unexpectedly leaping (with one hand dragging her unconscious mother) onto the top of something that resembled a monorail made out of pure white light. How she was able to hang on while this thing was travelling beyond light speed was another mystery.

"Thank God, I put a protection shield around us before we made the jump," she said to her mother who was floating beside her. If her mother heard her, she would have berated her for saying God's name in vain.

Her mother, oblivious to what was happening, slept on. She was more resilient than Cristal gave her credit for.

"If we come out of this alive," she said. "I promise to be nicer to you." She squeezed her hand in affirmation.

No more time to ponder. Their lives, or more importantly, their souls were at stake.

Time to assess the situation.

How was she going to get them back to Megiddo? Was that where she was supposed to go?

"Dear God," she prayed. "Please guide us to where You need us to be. Give us the strength to do Your Will."

At that moment, a giant snow globe flew by, whirring as it passed from behind, towards the direction the train was headed.

"Woah, that was close."

Another globe flew by, followed by another globe and another. In one globe, groups of men, women, some with small children, were shoving their way onto the ramp of what looked like a cruise ship. In another globe, there were more people clamoring onto another ship. Globe after globe contained scenes of ships filling up with people. It seemed each globe was from a different part of the world, the people from different ages and races.

"What is going on? Where are they going?" she asked herself.

"They are heading to Jerusalem," a deep voice replied.

She tightened her grip on her mother's hand while preparing to unleash her energy should she need to.

"Why?" she asked, trying not to let her voice waver.

"They believe that is where the prophecy will be fulfilled."

"Prophecy?"

"It's what you humans call it."

Something about the voice was hypnotic and familiar. Her gut was telling her not to trust it.

"Trust is an interesting concept," the voice continued.

She was about to respond when she felt her mother's hand

squeeze hers. She squeezed back, relieved that her mom was finally awakening from her comatose state.

Her mom squeezed her hand once more but this time more tightly.

"Raffe," she said in a tiny whisper.

Cristal guessed it was Raffe behind the voice. Logically, she should have been afraid of him, but a sense of calm had overcome her fear. *God would save them and that meant there'd be nothing to fear.*

"Trust," she replied to the voice, "is hard to give especially when it was broken before."

"Humans have such finite views of everything. What you may consider as broken is really collateral damage for the sake of the mission."

"So you consider us collateral damage?" Her words were only a distraction. She had to figure a way off this train.

"This 'train,' as you call it, is your one way ticket to Purgatory. Do not pass go. Do not collect two hundred dollars."

He must have been smiling at his attempt at humor.

"And who exactly told you that it's our time to go?"

A larger globe hovered before her.

She sighed. What was he trying to do now?

This globe materialized a horrific scene. A woman was holding a baby up in the air. It lay limp in her hands as she wailed. The view was blocked by a group of men waving to her. They led her off to the right side of the globe revealing the remains of rubble, black smoke and fires where an apparent explosion had turned what looked like a building into a pile of rubble. Pockets of people scrambled past. The scene moved sharply to the left.

She sucked in her breath.

What once was a large stone archway over an entrance sat in pieces on the ground, an arm and a leg protruding from underneath. On a large piece of rubble, one sign remained intact. It read "Global Nation University, New York."

CHAPTER 25
SAVE YOURSELF

Spread out on the kitchen table was a map where the creases crossed into the bright blue areas of Israel and the bold green of the new Palestine. The map was riddled with dried goods Walid had grabbed from his mother's cupboards. Hunched over the table, Aaron Doub waved a wooden ladle and tapped the map. Each item represented different factions of resistance groups.

"*Abu Harry*, did you want dried beans or dates in the city of Jerusalem?" Walid asked.

Harry found it strange to his ears to hear Walid refer to Aaron as 'father of Harry' in the traditional way Arabs addressed each other.

Aaron's brow arched sharply. "You, young man, of all people, should know which groups are moving towards the city of Jerusalem. Shame on you for not knowing!"

Walid threw Harry a look of frustration.

Navy beans represented resisters in Tel Aviv who left GN,

upset with the way the new government had taken control of every aspect of Israeli life. In an attempt to free themselves from endless scrutiny from GN, they cut out the microchips embedded in their arms and left the GN controlled areas. Piles of beans were scattered all over the map, reflecting the current situation.

Dried fruit represented the Israeli-Palestinian population. Unlike the Jewish sectors, the Arab sectors had remained relatively intact after the earthquake. Marked by economical hardship prior to the quake, Israeli-Palestinians prided themselves for not seeking assistance from GN, remaining self-sufficient after the quake.

When Walid ran out of dried goods, he took out the jars of nuts his mom stashed away only for special events. 'Just don't tell *Immee*, my mother," he said.

"Tell me what?" Walid's mother asked in Arabic as she entered the room.

Serena smirked, knowing that family drama was about to erupt.

"*Ma-fee ishi, Immee*. It's nothing, Ma," Walid said, pushing the jars further down the counter.

Aaron stepped forward with a huge smile on his face and opened his arms wide. "*Im Walid*, I enjoyed the meal very much. Very delicious! *Ekteer tayyib!*" he said in Arabic with a strong Hebrew accent.

Her nostrils flared briefly. It wasn't the first time the men in her life excluded her from their important discussions. Still, she wasn't as foolish or as ignorant as they deemed her to be. She flashed a polite smile in return. "*Sah-tain*. Double your good health."

She turned back to her son, narrowing her eyes as she

spoke. "You better not be doing something you'll regret, *Ebnee*, my son."

Walid leaned towards her. "*Akeed y'amma*. Of course, Ma," he said, gently kissing the top of her head, which was covered in a bronze colored hijab.

Not easily fooled, she pointed at the map. "The end is near and you think this is going to stop it. Why not join me in the salon for morning prayers instead? Praying to Allah is the only way to save our souls."

Harry glanced around the room before addressing *Im Walid*. "In fact, *Im Walid*, you speak the truth. It is written in the Koran that 'It is Allah Who takes away the souls of people at their death; and in their sleep, of those that have not died. Then He retains the souls of those against whom He had decreed death and returns those of others till an appointed time. In that indeed are signs for people who reflect.' Submitting to the Almighty God is indeed the only way to save our souls. From now on, we will join you for prayers."

Aaron's eyebrows shot up.

Walid beamed, his toothy smile stretching from ear to ear.

Serena came up to *Im Walid* and hugged her around her waist. "Yes, we will join you for prayers, *Im Walid*," she said.

Im Walid's eyes twinkled and she patted Serena on her arm. "Very good, *bintee*, my dear girl. You will sit with me later for coffee and dessert?" She spun towards Harry, her tone sharpening. "I expect that all of this will be put away in their proper places when you're all done, correct? All right, I will leave you all with your end of the world plotting. I will see what my daughters are up to."

When she left the room, Aaron waved his ladle in the air.

"Back to business, everyone." Without skipping a beat, he leaned forward towards the map. "We will use the nuts to represent those who refused to participate in the chip program. We know they escaped GN's heavy-handed governing and moved underground. Cashews will be Judaeo-Christian activists. Pistachios will be Orthodox Jews. Almonds can represent the secular resisters."

"Like what Walid's mom said. What is the point of all this?" Harry asked.

Aaron waved the ladle at him, his voice bellowing as if he were in a huge theater hall. "Last year, the imposter President Aaron Doub had made great strides to convince the world that he was their savior. In trying to win the hearts and minds of the human race, he had to accomplish more than any other leader in history. And in doing so, he managed, right here in the State of Israel, to cement the deal for the two-state solution that had long been proposed to end the Israeli-Palestinian conflict and bring peace to the Middle East."

Walid gave a grunt. "Two-state solution," he mumbled.

Harry threw him a glance.

Serena asked, "Walid, why didn't your family move to the new Palestine?"

He shrugged. "Why? This is our home, is it not?"

She gave him a nod. "Of course."

Walid looked back at Aaron. "Please continue, *Abu Harry*."

Taking the cue, Aaron gave a deep dramatic breath and began. "The natural disasters made all countries look inward. The destabilization of the world caused governments to seek GN for help. GN became the global governing body to bring order out of the chaos. So yes, the new Palestine is its own state on paper, but without the means to be self-sufficient, in fact, GN is the de facto ruler of the world."

"Thanks, dad, for updating us with something we didn't already know. Just tell Walid which ones should be in Jerusalem. Did you forget that we've got an archangel to save and Cristal to find?"

His father gave him a piercing look then pursed his lips. "You're right, my son. Time is of the essence." He tapped the map on the same spot and said, "Move all but the dates here."

Walid and Serena shot Harry a look.

Serena cleared her throat. "Mr. Doub, just to clarify, you want to move everything but the dates to Jerusalem? There won't be enough room."

Aaron's eyes lit up. He waved the ladle like a maestro conducting an orchestra. "Precisely, my dear!"

Harry leaned forward, putting both hands on the table. "Can you please explain what you mean?"

A smile crept onto Walid's face. "*Masboot*, right. They want to go to Jerusalem. It is in their Holy Books. *Nabu'a*. The what you call in Engleesh?"

Harry answered. "Prophecy."

"Ah yes, prophecy. They go to Jerusalem because of prophecy."

Aaron nodded like a proud father. "Very good, Walid. You answered correctly."

A smile flashed across Walid's face as he pushed all the dried goods over top of Jerusalem. The different piles overflowed over onto the surrounding regions. He gathered them into the pile only to watch them spill over again.

"Sorry, *Abu Harry*, these ones will not stay put."

Grinning from ear-to-ear, Aaron said, "See! You made my point!"

"What exactly is your point?" Harry shoved his chair back. "If it's true that all those people are going to Jerusalem because of some prophecy, then what does it have to do with us? If they want to kill each other over a piece of land, then that's their own prerogative. We need to focus on what is important for us."

Aaron crossed his arms over his chest, the ladle still in his grip. His eyes narrowed into accusing slits. "You have always been narrow-minded and self-serving. You never respected me as your father. I had hoped that this would be our second chance to mend our differences, but you don't want the olive branch I'm extending to you. You want to ignore my help and follow your own agenda even when I can provide concrete help."

Harry couldn't believe his ears. "Why don't you act like a father instead of lecturing me like a prof?"

Aaron stared at him, his nostrils flaring while the corner of his lip twitched. The ladle tapped the side of his arm in frenetic beats.

He could feel Serena shooting daggers with her eyes. 'Play nice with your father' she had pleaded with him before he had entered the kitchen. 'I'll play nice only because you asked' he had mumbled back.

Just then, Harry felt his bracelet vibrate against his wrist.

Aaron turned to his right and began speaking in Hebrew.

"I'm trying my best, but as you can see my stubborn son won't listen," he said, shaking his head. He paused, "What do you mean you want to take over? Oh no. You will not trick me this time. The last time you took over my body, you left me with horrible gas that took me days to release."

There he goes with his eccentricity again.

"Who is he talking to?" Walid asked, stifling a chuckle.

"Your guess is as good as mine," Harry said getting up. He nodded to Serena. "Can I have a word with you?"

"Sure."

They both slipped out of the kitchen into the dimness of the hallway.

"Did you get a notification too?" she asked.

"Yes, Cristal is trying to contact us."

He touched his bracelet and a small rectangular white light screen floated in front of them. The images were blurry at first until the shape of Cristal's face came up. Her lips were moving, but there was no audio.

"We can't hear you," he said gesturing his ear.

Serena stepped forward and motioned in sign language the same message.

Cristal nodded and closed her eyes.

"Can you hear me now?" her voice said in his head.

Serena gave a thumbs up.

"Yes, loud and clear," Serena replied.

"Where are you?" he asked.

"Purgatory."

"What?" Serena's eyes widened.

"I'm with my mother. I was trying to return her to the land of the living but I failed."

"How about you? Can you come back?" Serena asked.

"Raffe says my time is up and my destination is here."

Harry watched Cristal carefully. Her demeanor reflected a

calm serenity. Did the time in solitude at GN change her? Why was she accepting her fate so easily?

It was impossible to believe Almighty God would have given Cristal so much power only to be stuck in prison for twelve months and then end up in Purgatory.

"Your time and your mother's time are not up," he said. *"He is tricking you! We can help you come here. We need you. You have to believe. Cristal, you have to believe you are meant to fight with us. Don't give up now."*

Her eyes flickered open.

"There is so much despair here. My mother is suffering along with the others. I cannot leave her here."

He couldn't believe his ears. *"This isn't about her or about you. If it's her time, then so be it. But I refuse to believe it is your time. We need you here. Dear God Almighty, is it Your Will for Cristal to come back here?"*

The house shook in one violent wave. A clap of thunder exploded above them.

In the floating screen, Cristal's attention was diverted away, her gaze focusing upwards. She seemed to be speaking to someone. She clasped her hands together as if in prayer. She bowed her head and a blanket of white light fell upon her.

"No, don't take her!" he cried out.

"Cristal, don't go!" Serena yelled out loud.

The screen vanished.

The pain in his chest was crushing his ribs. Saving Cristal had all seemed doable way back when they were in New York. How gullible and naïve they'd been then. Kerim had provided them with spiritual training, but nothing could prepare them for this.

Serena crumpled onto the cold marble tile, her tiny body

heaving sobs. He knelt down and pulled her close to him, burying his face into her hair. Tears he detested burned his cheeks.

"I don't understand," she moaned into his shoulder. "How do we win this?"

Harry could sense Aaron and Walid's presence behind him.

A cold wind blew across and swirled around them in angry circles.

"Son, don't give up hope. It is now that your faith is going to be tested over and over. We will get your friend back. I promise you this."

His insides were churning and it was taking all his will to appear calm. He couldn't allow Serena to see him like this. He needed to lead, not fall apart.

"How can you promise me that?" he asked, brushing his face with his hand. He stood up and turned to face him.

Aaron and Walid were standing just beneath the archway of the kitchen. He was about to give his father a piece of his mind when he realized standing behind them were dozens of men dressed like his father, in long white robes. They would have been easily mistaken as local villagers except for the feathered wings folded on their backs.

"What is this?" he asked, stepping back.

Serena grabbed his elbow. "Gabriel said these are the angels who are going to help us."

Aaron pointed the ladle at both of them.

"Your faith is key," he said. "The Almighty has given humanity so many chances. He has time and time again almost wiped humans off the face of the earth. But because of the faith and humility from even the smallest number of people, he saves us over and over again. Have some faith, son. Out of all the things I give to you as your father, take this advice. Not just from me but from those here who are risking themselves to save humanity even when the hope of saving us seems bleak."

From the middle of the group, a tall figure moved towards them. The angels stepped aside to let him pass.

Walid looked over his shoulder, a huge smile stretching across his face.

"I did my best to take care of them," he said.

The dark-haired angel stood in front of them.

"You did a great job, Walid," he said, patting him on the shoulder.

His voice gave him away.

Serena let go of his arm and ran forward.

"Kerim! Thank God, you're okay!"

CHAPTER 26
PURGATORY

Cristal realized the lessons on Purgatory she picked up from her Catechism classes were more fairy tale than reality. Instead of lakes of brimstone and fire, Purgatory was a cold and sterile place similar to a hospital except the corridors were walls of cloud towering around them in a maze-like fashion. Above them, an incredible white light rained down, sending continuous static electric shocks on her skin. The pain reminded her of the one time Joanna had convinced her to go for an electrolysis hair removal session. She told her 'no decent guy is going to be turned on by your ape fur' after seeing her unshaven legs during weight training. What followed was thirty minutes of merciless agony while the clinician methodically zapped each strand of hair, pausing only to pat her hand and mumble, "it'll be over soon."

The zaps from the 'electric shocks' in Purgatory were as unpleasant, but her higher threshold for pain made it tolerable.

Raffe moved ahead of her, picking up his pace. She followed a short distance behind. After some time, he turned the corner, entering an open space where there were rows of thousands upon thousands of what looked like cylinders of concentrated light. Raffe led her between one of the rows. Inside the first cylinder, stood a middle-aged woman who looked past them as if watching something far into the distance. The woman called out, her hands motioning wildly.

Raffe continued forward in silence. Inside the next cylinder of light, stood a middle-aged man who also was gazing out into the distance.

As she looked further down, she realized all the cylinders of light were filled with human souls. Men and women of different races, sizes, cultures, all wearing the same woeful expression on their faces and uttering similar sounds of anguish and pain from their lips.

"What are they looking at causing them so much grief?" she asked.

Raffe did not pause or turn to address her. "Their sins," he said with a grunt.

Just then, a small dark man stepped out of one of the cylinders. She noticed outside the cylinder his body had become silvery and translucent.

"Help me, angel of God," he cried out.

To her surprise, Raffe stopped, stared into the man's eyes and placed his hand on top of his head.

"Trust in the Lord God Almighty," he said in a solemn tone. "Understand those here cannot enter the Kingdom of Heaven until they have purged themselves of all their mortal sins. Embrace this moment like your brothers and sisters around you. Now is the time to cleanse yourself for relief will soon be here."

The man looked up at him, a small glimmer of hope in his eyes. "Yes, I understand," he said as he stepped back into the stream of light. Once back in his spot, he shifted his gaze to the vision ahead of him. The tiny smile on his face faded and was replaced by a troubled look of sorrow.

Cristal was torn between the compassion Raffe had shown and the torment the souls were experiencing.

"You look upset," he said.

"I don't understand," she said. "Why does God want to torture these souls? Does He not see the pain this is causing them? Isn't He a loving God?" Tears welled up in her throat and she fought back the desire to weep.

"The Almighty is all loving and merciful. Souls must be cleansed before they can enter the serenity of Heaven. Does not a surgical team before preparing to perform surgery ensure they have scrubbed themselves and protected themselves from contaminating the sterility of the operating room? The cleansing is required for the good of each soul. Only after sin is purged from a soul, can they truly enjoy the company of Our Lord God. Does this help explain?"

She nodded even though the rationale didn't make much sense.

"Shall we continue?" he asked.

"Yes. Let's get this over with."

He turned and proceeded ahead of her. She tried her best to avoid looking into the columns of light as she passed but found herself drawn to them. How could she ignore the souls' presence when her senses were overwhelmed with their grief and sadness?

"Here we are," he said after several minutes. He slowed down and stopped at an empty cylinder of light. A woman was moving towards it, her body translucent with a shimmery glow along the edges.

A chill ran up her back when she recognized the woman was her mother.

"Everything is going to be all right," her mother said.

"What do you mean?" She shot Raffe a withering look of indignation. "Was this the mission?"

He crossed his arms over his chest and gave an impatient sigh. "My dear child, stop being overdramatic. Even your mother knows when the Almighty says it is time, it is time."

Cristal shook with rage. "You want me to believe God told you to bring us here? Why couldn't you just take her yourself when she was in Israel? Why have the big show of us impersonating Israeli guards and then teleporting us to Limbo, only to end up here?"

Olivia came up to her, her face glowing.

"My darling. It is my time and what has happened is what was meant to happen," she said in a soothing tone. "I realize I hadn't been a very good mother after your dad disappeared. After the earthquake, I pleaded with God to find you. He answered my prayers by bringing you to me."

"But are you sure it is your time? Did Raffe trick you to give your soul to him?"

He scowled and waved his hand. "Enough family drama. There are bigger things at hand. Olivia, please."

Cristal opened her mouth to argue, but her mother took her by the hand. "It's all right," she said. "I have many sins to repent for. Knowing Heaven awaits me is what gives me strength."

Her mother released her hand, turned and walked towards the empty column of light.

Cristal felt her pulse racing as a volcano of emotions churned inside.

Why must there be so much suffering? Was this what her mother would have to endure now? Although Olivia hadn't been the best mom, she had tried her best despite the circumstances.

Instinctively, she turned her gaze upwards and cried out, "Almighty God! I ask you dear Lord to forgive my mother for her sins and waive her from the pain of Purgatory."

Olivia blinked in disbelief.

Raffe chuckled to himself. "That is not how it works."

Cristal glowered at him. "I wasn't talking to you," she snapped.

He opened his mouth to berate her when from high above a thunderous sound, much like the one she heard the day of the earthquake in Akko, filled the air.

CHAPTER 27
LOWLY SERVANT

R affe's mouth opened to speak, but the sound of the winds made anything he might have said inaudible.

The cylinders of light jerked from side to side, awakening the souls from their mental suspension. Suddenly an explosion of light, so bright it made any other light seem like shadow, lit up the sky.

Raffe fell suddenly to his knee and bowed his head. Olivia and the other souls followed suit.

Every cell in her body shook. She collapsed on the ground on both knees.

A Voice, the sound of thunder, filled their ears. "My child, explain why your mother would be excused from purging her sins when so many others here are made to suffer?"

Every cell in her body was quivering by His Holy Presence. Yet remarkably, there was no fear. After all, wasn't the Almighty God a just and merciful God?

"Have mercy, Almighty God," she said. "It is true waiving

my mother while the others pay their dues is unfair. You are a righteous God and I am but a lowly servant."

Her heart ached, heavy with the remorse and pain exuding from surrounding souls. Flashes of memory, the torture she'd encountered at GN sprung to mind. Without the spiritual power and the blessings the Almighty God gave her, she wouldn't have survived. How could she allow this kind of torment on anyone?

After a deep breath, she said in a quiet voice. "I humbly ask you Lord God to allow me to do the penance for all the souls here today."

Raffe's head snapped up, his eyes wide with shock. Olivia reached out her hand to her, tears streaking down her cheeks.

The Voice of God thundered, "Do you know what you ask for, child?"

Cristal trembled. Ever since the day in Akko, when she had caused the huge earthquake and opened the spiritual portals, she knew deep inside her soul she had to do whatever it took to save humanity. Her own spiritual powers were a gift from the Almighty Himself and she understood what she had to do.

"Yes, dear Almighty God, I do." She shot her mom a glance before continuing. "I also ask You give mercy to my father Carlos Hernandez and Bina Schwartz. All they want to do is save humanity. They cannot do this if archangel Rafael continues hunting them."

The silence that followed was deafening. No one dared to move.

After the longest few minutes, ocean waves filled her ears and the Voice of God softened. "You ask for penance for sins you did not commit. Century upon century, humanity has shunned the prophets I have sent and have turned to worshipping evil instead. And yet there are a few who astound Me with their virtue and courage. Is it not these few who have saved humanity from decimation time and time again?"

Her breathing steadied as she absorbed His words.

After a brief pause, He said, "You shall receive what you ask for. Your sacrifice has saved the souls here this day."

Before Cristal could reply, the Heavenly light vanished.

Raffe rose slowly to his feet. He reached his hand and helped Olivia up.

The others followed suit and cautiously stepped out of their columns of light. A murmur grew among them.

"What is happening?" one asked.

"Is it true? Did this girl ask to take our punishment?"

Raffe raised his arms, the expression on his face fierce. "Did you not hear the Almighty God? Not one of you deserves what this child has asked for! She is free from mortal sin and yet she has given the ultimate sacrifice."

His words echoed around them.

Olivia ran up to Cristal, her arms outstretched as she pleaded. "I can't allow you to do this. No, I will do my penance."

Some souls were frozen with fear, while others said, "He's right. How can we face God if we did not do our penance for our own sins?"

A few of them scrambled back into their columns of light. Others looked bewildered.

"But God told us she would take our punishment which means we can go to heaven."

Cristal stood by Raffe, a formidable archangel, whose shoulders slumped like a man about to concede defeat.

"Never thought you had a good word to say about me," she said.

Raffe made a grimace. "When I was given this mission, I was told you were special. But I wasn't willing to believe that of a mortal, much less a child. You have proven me wrong."

"Promise you'll take care of my parents, Bina, Kerim, Gabriel, Harry, and Serena for me, will you?"

His eyes widened and a hint of a tear slid down his cheek. "Yes, I promise you," he said with a soft grunt.

"I didn't know angels could cry," she said softly.

He swiped his cheek with his hand and looked away. "I'm in human form and can't control the automatic reflex of the autonomic nervous system."

"Whatever you say," she said, touched by his rare show of emotion.

She felt the gaze of the souls upon her. Her mother's hands covered her face as she wept.

One thing left to do. Cristal closed her eyes and prayed 'Dear God, give me the strength to do Your Will," before stepping into the empty column of light.

CHAPTER 28
SIN

Smells of pumpkin spice and turkey drippings combined with odors of rotting floorboards and musty wallpaper filled her senses. Someone was mauling her neck and his hands were up her blouse. Cristal tried to push back but realized she couldn't. The body she was in wasn't hers.

'*Ding-dong!*' chimed the doorbell.

"Stop," she said in a raspy voice, gently pushing him away.

"Ignore it," he said. "No porch light means no candy." Pressing his face onto hers, he lodged his tongue inside her mouth. Cristal wanted to throw up even though the person she was in was enjoying every sick sweaty moment.

'*Ding-dong! Ding-dong!*'

"Drex, it might be your kids."

"It's not them. They're not gonna be back for at least an hour," he mumbled between kisses.

"What if it's your wife?" she asked.

"She has a key and she's across town with her sick mother. Stop killin' the mood, Lenora," he snapped.

⚜

IT HAD ALL STARTED AS A DARE. IT WAS THE YEAR LENORA had turned sixteen. Babysitting her neighbor's kids kept her busy and put spending money in her pocket. She was an only child; her dad was long gone before she could walk. Her mother worked double shifts to keep food on the table. Too tall for her age and slightly buck-toothed, the kids at school treated her like the alien she always felt she was.

This job was in some ways her escape from reality. The babysitting job opportunity came when Mrs. Jameson's mother was sent to live in a care home across town after suffering a stroke.

Lenora couldn't remember exactly when she came up with the idea. She'd daydreamed of her first kiss ever since she started reading romance novels.

The opportunity arrived when she met the neighbor's husband, Mr. Jameson. In his middle thirties with thinning hair and sporting a small beer gut, he definitely wasn't a heart throb. Despite the minor flaws, he was heaps more manly than any of the boys in her class. She plotted and planned how, when and where. But the timing never was right.

One day, Mrs. Jameson had left early to visit her mother at the hospital; the kids were in the family room watching television and Mr. Jameson had just come home, exhausted and moody. Usually, he'd tell her to go home, but this time he'd asked her to stay an extra hour. He needed to crash for a bit on the couch.

She remembered kneeling beside him, the cheap carpet felt scratchy against her knees. His chest rose up and down in gentle waves. He looked like a child, innocent and manly all at the same time. Her heart raced while her stomach was in knots. She leaned in close, so close she could smell his breath, sour and foul from his pack-a-day smoking habit.

No more excuses. She pressed her lips against his with determination and waited. For what exactly, she didn't know. Where were the fireworks, she'd read about in the romance novels? She sat back on her knees unsure of what to do next. It had been too easy.

Until his eyes snapped open.

Scrambling to her feet, she dashed for the front door.

"Wait," she heard him say.

She grabbed her jacket from the coat rack. "Gotta go," she mumbled.

"I said, wait."

She felt his hands on her shoulders. He spun her around with force and the next thing she knew his mouth was pressing against hers, his tongue probing hers with eager curiosity. *Still no fireworks but it was definitely different.*

And so it began, her grownup "affair" with the next-door neighbor's husband. Yes, he was a married man and technically married to her boss. But heck, she reasoned, it was just kissing and touching. Nothing more. Really wasn't that bad of a sin. His wife was never around to take care of her husband or her kids. Lenora was doing her a favor for filling in.

However, this Hallowe'en night the sin she started reared its ugly head and demanded payback.

That night, groping and kissing didn't seem to be enough for Mr. Jameson.

"I want more," he breathed into her hair.

'Ding-dong! Ding-dong!'

"Really, we should check to see if it's the kids."

He shoved her hard against the couch and cussed under his breath.

"Fine."

She watched as he stomped to the front door and peeked through the peephole.

"Go away! Porch light ain't on. So no candy!" he yelled.

❦

EARLIER THAT DAY, MRS. JAMESON HAD COME HOME AND was in the meanest of moods. She snapped at the children and then locked herself in her room. Later, she'd emerged, her eyes red-rimmed as if she'd been crying. Lorena asked her if she needed any help.

"You've helped more than enough" was the response. Mrs. Jameson opened her purse, took out a handful of cash and handed it to her. "Here, this will cover this month and two extra months as severance."

"Severance?"

"You're fired. Get your stuff and go."

"But I promised to bring the children trick-or-treating."

"Get out. Now."

Lorena left without saying goodbye to the kids. *How dare she fire her after all she did to help with her children?* She later sulked in her room, wishing dreadful things upon her ex-boss.

The ringing of the phone interrupted her angry thoughts. Mr. Jameson's voice on the other end was a pleasant surprise.

"Come over," he'd said.

"Your wife fired me," she'd said.

"Yeah, so what? I want to see you. Not asking you to babysit. Things are gonna be different around here from now on."

The twins were out trick-or-treating he told her and the little one was asleep in her crib. It seemed all-wrong, but the thrill of having him to herself was enticing.

❧

HE STUMBLED BACK TO THE COUCH.

"Told you, it's just a bunch of kids who don't get the rules. No light. No candy."

"I don't want your wife to walk in on us," she said.

He grabbed her just then. Yanked her up actually. She tried to steady herself, her feet slipping on the carpet. He pulled her to her feet and began pushing her down the hall.

"What's going on?" she asked. He'd never been this rough before.

He started mumbling crazy stuff. "She thinks she can leave me. After all I've done for her."

Playing house had been Lenora's intention from the start. What began as a simple dare was suddenly turning into a nightmare.

"Please stop. You're hurting me."

Half dragging her, he threw open the door to the master bedroom. It was the only room in the house she hadn't been allowed to enter.

The room wasn't what she had imagined. Dark, dank and crammed with old furniture, the shadows on the wall danced with the flickering candlelight.

He opened another door and shoved her inside. Her feet stepped on cold tile and she stumbled forward in the darkness. The smell of vomit and urine hit her nose making her want to heave.

She heard a click and the lights lit up the room.

"This is what you started, little girl," he growled in her ear.

Staring back at her was Mrs. Jameson sprawled naked in the bathtub, her chest carved open like a turkey on Thanksgiving Day.

Cristal felt a scream, an earth-shattering cry, rip through Lenora's soul. She realized she too had screamed with her, the wave of the girl's horror and fear colliding and melding into Cristal's own self awareness.

CHAPTER 29
THE RESURRECTED

The impromptu gathering on the street below Walid's home had been brought on earlier by the piercing sound of a trumpet blast which was unlike any sound Harry had ever heard before.

Harry recalled seeing the grim look on Kerim's face and how the angels scrambled towards him saying the time was upon them.

From their view on the veranda overlooking the street below, they watched the villagers question Kerim and the angels while Harry's father stood off to the side, his mouth opening at times as if to intervene. Walid was observing at street level, a short distance from the commotion just inside the property's gate. The villagers didn't seem to notice they were surrounded by angels or perhaps they couldn't see their wings, Harry reasoned to himself.

Walid's sister, Shaima, said to her younger sisters in

Arabic, "Maybe more people have disappeared. That sounds like the same trumpet sound. I'm sure of it."

Serena turned to her. "You've heard this before?"

Shaima's face lit up. "Yes! Right before the earthquake, we heard it. That's when they disappeared."

"You mean when they went missing?"

She raised her chin and scrunched her chubby cheeks in a pout. "No, I mean disappeared. We saw friends and loved ones disappear right before our eyes. The neighbours said they heard this happen outside our village too."

Nazreen, the middle sister, added softly, "What she says is true. And the night when we heard the trumpet, I heard *Immee,* my mother, and Walid arguing about the first trumpet."

"First trumpet?" Harry and Serena said in unison.

"Aywah! Yes!" Nazreen called out, excited to see she had her guests' attention. "Walid had asked *Immee* about the first trumpet. He said he remembered hearing it when he was a little boy but couldn't remember if disappearances had happened then."

Shaima's eyebrows shot up. "Walid heard a trumpet sound before?"

Nosayba, the youngest, jumped up and down and clapped her hands, her dark curls bouncing on her shoulders. "*Ahu-ee Walid*, my brother Walid hears trumpets!"

Nazreen's emerald coloured eyes darkened as she continued. "*Immee* got upset and told Walid she didn't remember any trumpet sound and that he must have been mistaken."

Before she could finish her story, they were interrupted by the villagers' voices which had grown louder. "*Rowwah min hone!* Get away from here! You are not welcome!"

Walid's mother rushed from inside the house onto the veranda. "The people are demanding Aaron leave the village immediately."

"Why?" Serena asked.

"They believe he's the *dajjal* sent to take the village away from us again."

"*Im Walid*, I think you're mistaken," Harry said. "My father isn't the false messiah. And what do you mean by 'take the village away again?'"

"Hm?" Walid's mother lifted her chin as if she hadn't heard him.

"You said, '…take the village away from us again?'"

Her lips pressed together, shaking her head as she walked by them. "I need to help sort this out."

She clamored down the stairs, the heels of her sandals making a soft thud against the stone steps. She moved rather swiftly for someone with her compact stature and wide girth. Without a pause, she raced across the cemented yard and through the metal gated door, pushing Walid to the side as she passed him.

"What was that about?" Serena asked.

He shrugged. "Is it just me or does she seem like she's being evasive?"

"You mean, like the story about Walid's father? When Cristal and I were here right after the earthquake, she told us that he died a long time ago. But last night, I heard her say 'when Walid's father left' and then she corrected herself right afterwards. She corrects herself a lot. Maybe she's losing her memory?"

The older sister crossed her arms over her chest. "*Immee* has the memory of an elephant! She can remember every

child's name and birth date of every neighbor in our village
and all the names of the villagers and their cousins' cousin."

Nazreen nodded in agreement while Nosayba, the little
one, jumped up and down. "*Immee* is an elephant!"

Shaima patted Nosayba on the head and giggled. "No,
that's not right, silly. Don't let *Immee* hear you."

Nazreen pulled Harry's elbow and pointed over the
railing.

"*Immee* might be in danger!"

In the middle of the dusty street, *Im Walid* stood with her
arms on her hips between the angels and the villagers who
towered over her. One of the older villagers, a tall wiry man
who had been waving his arms at Kerim, stepped towards her.

"That's the mayor," whispered Nazreen.

"You have allowed this to happen!" he cried out, wagging
his finger at Walid's mother.

"This is not for us to decide," she said in a low voice.

He waved his arm towards Harry's father. "First your
husband brings this one here. *Abu Walid* promised us it was
only temporary."

Shaima sucked in her breath and clutched Nazreen's
shoulder. "What is he saying? Our father is dead. How can
this be?"

The mayor continued. "We have tried to live a quiet life.
Allah, the Compassionate, the Merciful, returned us here to
live our lives in peace."

Im Walid raised her chin, her stance unwavering. "Do you
not believe Allah resurrected us to help be the arm of
His Will?"

The other villagers, men and women, young and old
murmured to each other in hushed tones.

"What if what she says is true?" an older woman asked her husband.

"She and her husband have only brought trouble here," a man said.

A stout man pointed at Harry's father. "I knew hiding that false messiah in our midst would bring God's army of angels here."

"But what if this means we are to help fight HaShem's war?"

"What if these are not sent by Allah but by the false messiah himself?"

"The Almighty God will protect us!"

Harry and Serena exchanged looks as Shaima and Nazreen scrambled closer to the balcony railing to listen.

"What does HaShem and God mean?" Nosayba asked, tugging at her older sisters' t-shirts.

Nazreen pulled her close and kissed her rosy cheek. "Both words refer to Allah. HaShem is how the *Yahudi*, the Jews, call Allah. And God is how the *ajanibiin Masahiyin*, the Christian foreigners, call Allah."

Nosayba smiled widely exposing her tiny teeth. "*Akeed*, of course! I knew that."

One of the angels raised his voice. "Do you dare question our intentions?"

"Was it not us who returned you to Megiddo?" another asked.

The other angels and villagers began joining in with shouts and raised fists.

Kerim raised his hand up silencing the crowd.

"The Almighty Father has called all who are the true believers in Him to fight the false messiah. Although this man

165

looks like the president of Global Nation, he is definitely not the false messiah. This man beside me is simply a man."

Aaron raised his bushy eyebrows, made a scowl and crossed his arms over his chest. "Not just simply any man," he mumbled.

Kerim's eyes narrowed briefly before continuing. "The president of GN is the false messiah and he is impersonating this man. You of the resurrected are destined to join the Almighty's army and destroy the anti-christ."

Serena grabbed Harry by the shoulder. "They keep saying 'resurrected'? Did I hear that right? Doesn't that mean 'raised from the dead'?"

He nodded while he tried to comprehend what was unfolding before them.

The mayor stepped in front of Kerim. His slight figure appeared more fragile in contrast to the archangel's solid frame, but his voice bellowed like a man ten times his size. He said in Arabic, "Not all of you know this. We have kept our silence in order to keep the peace. But I cannot be silent anymore.

"Sixty eight years ago, my family and neighbors were cast out of our village of Lajjun and forced to live in the neighboring one. Others came and made a kibbutz on our lands. We were not warriors, just simple farmers and so we accepted our fate.

"It was one like you who came to me in a dream. An angel of God who said one day I will be asked to return to this village and wait for His Word. And so I waited just like the others here. We lived our lives, raised our children for thirty more years but no word came. But still I waited until the day I died."

Shaima sucked in her breath again. "What is he saying? What does he mean?" She shoved Nazreen aside and pressed her face between the railing hoping to get a better view.

Harry grabbed Serena's hand while his heart pounded in his chest. God's overall plan was much more than they could comprehend.

The mayor turned and addressed the villagers.

"It was the sound of the first trumpet which awoke me from my grave. I found myself wandering the streets wondering to myself if this was Heaven. My surroundings seemed familiar and yet they weren't. The streets were filled with the noise of the automobiles and the smell of gasoline. It was the same as I had left it but much more louder and dirtier.

"It was like being in a dream. One minute I was walking on one street and the next I found myself standing at my house. I walked inside relieved to be home but aware things weren't right. The furniture was different, the paint was different and I didn't recognize all the pictures on the wall. Then I heard voices coming from the kitchen. I could hear my oldest son speaking to my wife. I hurried into the room hoping to wake up from the nightmare I was in. Indeed, it was my wife and son standing in the kitchen, except they were now much older than I remembered. They welcomed me as one would welcome a stranger. My wife asked, 'Are you the neighbor's grandson visiting from Germany?' 'It's me, your husband!' I cried out. Her face twisted in shock and my son lunged at me. 'Who are you? My father died ten years ago.'

"Died, ten years ago? How could my wife and my son not recognize me? It was not until I saw myself in a mirror later on did I realize I appeared years younger, much like when I was in my early forties. I gasped when I saw the calendar on the wall which said it was in fact 1988, a decade more than it should have been."

The others nodded in agreement. The woman who had spoken earlier said, "I recall the car accident which took my life and then later waking up and wandering Kafr Kana in a daze. I saw my reflection in a shop window and was shocked I was looking at myself but as a young girl before I was married. It was a miracle."

A short man at the back of the crowd lifted his fist. "Miracle? Yes, we returned from the dead, but what good came of it? Our original family and friends didn't recognize us and shunned us like we were deranged people."

The woman turned around to him.

"But don't you remember these angels sent *Abu* and *Im Walid* to us and they brought us here to the safety of the village of Lajjun in Megiddo? If it were not for them and our neighboring friends from the kibbutz, we wouldn't have been able to settle and lead a peaceful new life."

A man and woman dressed in t-shirts and jeans stepped forward.

In Hebrew, the man said, "*Slicha*, sorry to interrupt. My wife and I also returned here thirty years ago. Before that, we lived in Tel Aviv as husband and wife into our seventies until we died, just days apart from each other. We do recall hearing the trumpet and found ourselves walking the streets of Tel Aviv but decades younger in age than when we had died.

"We sought answers too. We had no identification, no money, nothing but the clothes on our backs. Our families and friends didn't believe our stories. Instead they sent the police to take us to the hospital for mental examinations.

"We are grateful God allowed us to lead a new life with our wonderful friends here and give us a chance to raise a family again. If it weren't for *Abu* and *Im Walid*, we would have had nowhere to go. They were the ones who managed to get us identity cards and other government resources. I say if God is calling us to fight the Evil One, then we and our children will join you."

The man who had raised his fist pushed himself forward to the front of the crowd. "But my question is why? Some of us originally are from the Christian quarter of Bethlehem. I did not have an angel come speak to me and yet I am here returned from the dead. Some of our Jewish and Muslim friends did not encounter a visit from an angel of God when they first returned from the dead. We see the angels here today. These same angels who told some of you to wait for God to summon us to fight. You told us to wait so we waited. Waited years. *Abu Walid* told us to start our lives over and we did. We wed, had children and made new lives here. But now I am too old to fight. Many of us who returned from the dead feel the same way!"

Some villagers cried out. "*Masboot*! That is right!"

A stout woman wearing a dark hijab near the front raised both arms and said loudly, "*Mishan Allah*, for God's sake, I am in my sixties now. I have *sukkar* (diabetes). I am on medications and can hardly travel much less fight a war against the *dajjal*, the false messiah."

"She's right!" some cried out.

Kerim looked at the crowd, his gaze scanning the faces of all who were there. He spoke then in a voice which shook the ground and buildings and caused the winds to stir the dust into the air.

"I serve the Lord God Almighty. He asks me to call upon you to serve His Will. Have you forgotten what He has done for you? I cannot force you to fight as the Almighty has given you free will. But do not be mistaken. For the Day of Judgment is near. When each one of you stands before Him to be judged, how will you explain your actions?"

Blackened clouds rolled overhead while bolts of lightning split the sky followed by tumultuous thunder claps which shook the earth.

Kerim closed his eyes and said, "The time has come. Walk with me to the mount of Megiddo, those of you who wish to serve the Lord God Almighty."

CHAPTER 30
CLOSING OF PURGATORY

C ristal opened her eyes and found herself standing in a white small space. Sensing Raffe's presence beside her, she spoke, relieved to to be able to hear her own voice again.

"That was an awful experience," she said.

"Purging of sins is not meant to be pleasant," he replied.

"Not sure what to say. I literally did nothing to help the girl."

"Your willingness to witness in itself is what has moved the Almighty. Your self sacrifice is all that matters," Raffe said in a solemn tone.

She turned to face him, her mind spinning in circles. "Have I become desensitized? I didn't have any sorrow for her."

He dropped his gaze to his hands. "Perhaps."

"I really don't get this place. I don't want to question God's purpose, but I wonder if I've messed things up with my crazy ideas."

He stood up and pushed the wall open. "Come with me."

She followed him into another space. In the corner stood a tall middle aged woman with brilliant white hair. Her face was long and sallow, her eyes dark like marbles.

There was no need for introductions.

"Lenora," she said.

The woman nodded, her eyes filling with tears.

"I wish I could say the sins of my youth were the last. I tried to think I lived a better life after what happened to poor Mrs. Jameson. But looking back, I realize how weak and self-centred I was for most of it. When my mother became sick, I sent her to a home even when I vowed never to. In the end, she died alone.

"Instead of finding happiness, I drowned myself in self-pity. I self-medicated on pills and alcohol. I spoiled my children and they grew to be selfish. They moved on as soon as they were old enough. Eventually, my husband left. He told me he could barely stand me anymore. Looking back, I know I deserved that.

"I sank deeper into my own self-made misery. I was taking pills and alcohol to drown out the pain. I woke up in the hospital one fateful day in the addiction recovery ward where a battle axe of a nurse was assigned to me. She hid my pills despite the doctor's orders to wean me off. She didn't believe in modern day docs' methods of babying patients instead of dealing with the addiction. She asked me if I wanted to be cured. I told her yes. She asked if I believed in God. I said, of course. In her rough manner, she declared, 'Well it's simple then. I must force the demons out of you.'

"It was a brutal few months. In the end, not only did I rid myself of my addictions, I found my faith in God. The nurse and I became very good friends. I volunteered at the hospital helping others recover from their addictions. I reconnected with my husband, mending our relationship over the years as friends. He helped me get back on my feet financially. When he fell ill, I took care of him until he passed away. Many years after, my nurse friend became sick and I cared for her until the day she died.

"I realized my purpose in life was to help others. I spent the rest of my days, volunteering and sitting with the sick and dying, consoling them and teaching them about our Savior."

Raffe moved in front of her and touched her forehead. "Are you sorry for your sins?"

Her eyes closed. "Yes, I am sorry for my sins and I pray to God Almighty for His forgiveness."

A blanket of light fell upon her as Raffe removed his hand from her head. Cristal felt a heavenly presence with them.

Lenora who had been wrought with worry began to relax. A smile crept upon her lips as if she were listening to something serene. Her body began transforming into a radiant glow.

Her eyes flickered open and she cried out. "The Almighty told me I'm forgiven. He said I am ready to go to the next part of my journey."

Lenora, now a heavenly body, was a glimmer of her human self with the semblance of her physical features almost holographic beneath the radiant glow.

"Thank you, dear child," she said to Cristal. "Before you came, I was consumed by fear and doubt. When you told God Almighty you would do the penance for all the souls, I realized how foolish I was for being afraid. It was very clear to me at that moment allowing someone else to do what I needed to do myself defeated the whole purpose of Purgatory. You opened our eyes. All the others feel the same way."

Cristal leaned towards Raffe and whispered, "What does she mean?"

Instead of answering, he pushed with one hand against the wall facing them. She marveled at how the surface of the wall melted away like frozen lace upon his touch. With both hands, he pushed against the side walls, his muscular arms extending beyond their visible length. The walls fell away leaving them standing in a large open space. Standing before them were hundreds of thousands of souls which had transformed, just like Lenora, into heavenly bodies.

"To answer your question, it was your mother who convinced these souls to do their own penance," Raffe said. "Like Lenora said, it would not have been the same if they had not purged themselves of their sins."

"My mother?"

He gave his customary grunt. "Is that not what I said?"

She scanned the faces of the souls in search of Olivia.

"Where is she?" she asked, after not finding her.

Her mother's voice entered her head. "I am here, Cristal."

She whirled around. "Where are you? I can't see you."

"Do not be afraid. I am now on the next part of the journey to meet our Maker."

Cristal swallowed the lump lodged in her throat. "I still don't understand."

"You and I played a part in helping the Almighty God."

"How? I still don't get it."

"Your sacrifice changed Purgatory. You opened the eyes of the souls which has brought upon God's compassion."

"I only did what I thought was the right thing to do."

"Exactly. There was no other reason than your desire to do what is good and right. Although I wasn't the best mother, I think I taught you well."

"I'm sorry I wasn't a better daughter."

A soft gentle laugh met her ears. "You will always be my baby girl. Now you must return to the land of the living. You must bring together your father and your friends. The Almighty God says it is time to prepare for the battle of all battles."

"How about you? Why aren't you coming?"

"Almighty God says you must go with Raffe. My work here is done. Don't worry. There will be a time when we will see each other again."

Before she could reply, she heard a *woosh* sound and felt her mother's presence leave her.

Her mother, the woman with whom she had just become closer to, was gone. Her heart ached, the little girl inside, longing to enjoy a few more moments with her mother. But just like everything else in her life, there was no time to reflect on it.

Her thoughts were interrupted by the cries of the souls calling out to her.

"Thank you for offering to do our penance," said a dark woman with a smile as bright as the glow around her.

"Your sacrifice will never be forgotten," said a man Cristal recognized from earlier.

"Your sacrifice opened our eyes," another one said.

"When we accepted our fate, we realized how compassionate God is. Because of you, He has eased the suffering," said another.

Raffe gave another grunt. Clapping his hands, he bellowed, "Enough talk! It is time!"

They scrambled to find their place in line among rows and rows of others.

"It's time!" someone said.

"It's finally happening!" another cried out.

"We're going to heaven!"

Their joy was infectious. Even Raffe had to hold back a chuckle before clapping his hands once again.

"May God be with you on the next part of your journey," he said.

Some souls lifted their hands upwards while others began waving. They were off to Heaven presumably the final stop of their journey.

"Godspeed," Cristal said under her breath, half wishing she could join them.

The ground beneath them swayed while a high pitched sound filled the air. The souls faded away row by row. She watched in amazement as hundreds of thousands of souls disappeared before her eyes.

Raffe remained resolute during the exodus.

She asked, "Will there be more souls arriving here?"

His expression hardened. "The third trumpet signalled the next phase. The remaining souls on Earth and in Limbo will be judged on the day of judgment. Purgatory is now closed."

She shuddered. "Is it okay to be afraid?"

He heaved a sigh. "Fear not and have faith in the Commander-in-Chief, the Almighty God. Has not all things come to pass as He has said? He is the Alpha and the Omega."

His words settled her anxious thoughts.

"You're right. Faith in the Almighty," she said with conviction.

"Does this mean I won't have to drag you kicking and screaming?"

She threw him a grin. "Very funny. I've never been dragged anywhere and where I go is because I will it."

His nostrils flared as he held back a smile. "True. You've been quite amenable for a human despite the bombardment of truths you've been forced to deal with in such a short amount of time. Are you ready now to embark on the next part of your mission?"

"Ready whenever you are," she said without hesitation.

"*Sababa*! Excellent," he said. He waved his arms in a dramatic upward motion and called out the secret words for teleportation.

"*Yallah!* Let's go!"

She couldn't help but smirk. The secret code she'd tried to use to escape Bezel's wrath at GN had been switched from Hebrew to Arabic. Obviously Raffe had intended for her not to escape.

A sudden wind rushed towards them, sweeping them up on top of a giant invisible tidal wave.

"Dear God help us," she said under her breath.

CHAPTER 31
DAY OF THE THIRD TRUMPET

On the Day of the Third Trumpet, the Resurrected were to accompany the archangel Kerim with the angels to the mount of Megiddo. Every night since, Nazreen would relive the events of that day in her visions and dreams.

She remembered when, right after Kerim's announcement, Walid, her brother, had stepped back into their courtyard with his head down, his face as white as a ghost.

"Walid, you will come with us," Kerim called from outside their gate.

Harry, who'd been standing beside her on the veranda, hurried down the steps. He stopped a few feet away from Walid when her mother entered the courtyard.

Walid's eyes widened as he turned to their mother. "*Immee*, mother, I do not understand."

She came to him and grabbed both of his hands, searching his eyes for acceptance. "*Ebnee*, my son, when you asked me about the first trumpet, I did not answer you truthfully. *Abuk*, your father, and I had promised to protect you from the truth until the time was right."

"Is it true then? Is *abuee*, my father, alive?" His chest heaved and tears welled up in his eyes. "*Ley?* Why did you lie to us?"

Im Walid cast her eyes down, her voice trembling as she spoke. "The angels told us to follow Allah's instructions. We were not to let the children know. We were not to discuss our past lives."

Walid shook his head, unable to grasp what he was hearing. "My sisters surely cannot be resurrected. I remember when they were born. I am so confused."

Kerim turned his gaze on them. "Walid, I will give you and your mother a few moments. It is a lot to absorb, I know. But I must remind you of the urgency." He waved for the angels to gather the Resurrected together.

Im Walid's eyes were red-rimmed, her lips a grim line.

"I have had sleepless nights since the day of the earthquake. Raffe is the archangel Rafael. He has visited us on numerous occasions. He brought Aaron to the village and told your father it was our mission to protect him. Your father was ordered by Raffe to return to Global Nation Tel Aviv to infiltrate the demons' secret plans. When he didn't come home, everyone assumed he had gone 'missing' like your brother Sami. Raffe ordered me to say he had died to stop the gossip. He recently warned me soon I'd have to tell you about our past. But now that it is time, *saeb ekteer*, it's very difficult."

Her body shook as she spoke, the tears streaming down her cheeks. She continued without pausing.

"*Abuk*, your father has been working with the Israeli government and Global Nation Tel Aviv first as a soldier, later moving up the ranks to a General in the Israeli Army from the time you were a little boy. He has been helping the Resurrected ones by using his connections in government to provide them with the proper papers and resources needed to keep their Israeli citizenship and status. How else could we have survived? We, the Resurrected, never spoke about our past to each other or to anyone.

"Fortunately, the Almighty provided the land for us to grow our own food and keep our farm animals. He blessed our friends in the neighboring kibbutz and they helped provide us with food and things to trade with each other. This is how we managed to survive this long."

The sisters were so entranced by their mother's story, they hadn't noticed Serena come down the stairs. She stood beside her *jozha*, her husband, Harry. The couple were listening intently to *Im Walid*.

"*Eib aleik*, shame on you! This is a private conversation," Shaima hissed under her breath. Although Nazreen was the only one who could hear her, she understood her sister's words were directed at their guests.

Walid turned his head away. "So you and father have come back from the dead?"

Im Walid reached up and touched Walid's cheek.

"What I'm about to say is something your father and I have kept in our hearts all these years. When you were five years old, you became very ill. The doctors told us it was a virus which they said you would recover from. But a fever fell upon you which would not go down. We rushed you to the *mustashfa*, hospital. The doctors tried everything. We prayed and prayed. You passed away in my arms in the middle of the night a few days later."

Walid stood frozen, his face hardened like granite. Nazreen and Shaima held each other, sobbing as they watched their mother reach out to hug their brother.

"Is that all, *Imee?*" he asked, his voice thick with emotion.

Their mother dropped her arms and folded her hands. She continued the story, her voice softening as if she were reliving the moment.

"I fell into a deep sadness which your father was unable to bring me out of. I too came down with the illness and died not long after."

Walid gazed past his mother and said in a soft voice, "I remember the trumpet. I remember holding your hand as we walked the streets. You were scared, I could hear it in your voice. '*Ya Allah sa'edna*, God help us,' you kept saying over and over."

Im Walid's eyes reddened as she fought back tears. She said, "When I heard the trumpet, I found you in my arms, alive and well. Thank God! The only thing I could think of was to bring you home. When your father saw us, he dropped down on his knees and he praised God. He told me an angel had visited him the night before. The angel had told him his mission was to help the Resurrected and that his son and wife would return to him."

Shaima gasped. "Walid and *Immee* returned from the dead?"

Nazreen was just as shocked, but something inside her remained calm. She had often wondered why she had encountered many dreams and visions all her life. Her mother never seemed surprised when she would tell her. Shaima used to tease her endlessly which made her shy to share with others, but her mother always listened and even encouraged her to elaborate.

Harry and Serena walked past Walid and their mother towards Kerim who was standing outside the gate.

"We are coming with you," Harry said in English.

Nazreen and Shaima had learned the language at school but were far from fluent. Ever since their mother had welcomed the English speaking guests to their home, they were able to pick up the basic language easily and were eager speaking it. However when serious topics filled with difficult and strange sounding words came up, they found themselves lost in translation.

Kerim turned to Harry. "Aaron is to stay here. It may be better if you and Serena remain with him here."

Serena shook her head, placing her hand on her hip. "No, you trained us to fight. You need our help."

"She's right, you know," Harry said. "Technically, I am resurrected too. Trust me, I haven't forgotten."

Shaima turned to Nazreen. "Does 'resurrected' mean come back from the dead?"

Nazreen shrugged. "Hush, I want to hear what they're saying."

Kerim raised an eyebrow, a small grin crossing his lips. "You have a point there. Although turning back time to bring you back to life may not be the same definition as resurrected, I'm not going to argue on a technicality."

He turned back to Walid and their mother. "It is time. Say your goodbyes."

CHAPTER 32
WALID'S SISTERS

The house was still and the dry heat hung over them, stifling their thoughts. It was only the three of them now. Everything about their lives changed on the Day of the Trumpet. Nazreen knew things would never be the same.

"When will we see you again?" Shaima had asked their mother unable to contain her despair.

Their mother said, "Be strong. Take care of Nosayba and each other. Pray for Allah's guidance and blessings."

Her brother Walid said, "*Inshallah*, God willing, we will see each other again, but we don't know if it will be here or in Paradise."

Shaima's shrill screams echoed across the village when the reality had finally sunk in. Being the middle child, Nazreen had been the calm one. Although, she too wanted to pull her hair and wail with her older sister, someone had to do what Allah had intended for them to do.

Weeks passed and the anguish over the departure of their mother and Walid had dulled to a numb pain. The deep wound was ripped open again when their dear little sister disappeared.

Nazreen wiped away a tear. She hated drifting into her thoughts. "*Bekefeh*, enough," she mumbled under her breath.

She sprinkled zaatar spice into the bowl of olive oil and gave it a quick stir. Her older sister had decided for the morning meal they would make *manakeesh*, baked bread topped with goat cheese and spices. Their mother always said 'good food lightens the spirits.'

Despite her initial protest, Nazreen soon warmed up to the idea. Allah the Almighty had willed this adversity upon them so it was her duty to embrace and make the most of it.

Nazreen tried to smile when Shaima brought the tray of flattened dough balls towards her. "*Ibtid zakaree*, remember when Serena called *manakeesh* personal pan pizzas?" she asked.

Nazreen heard a grunt and glanced over at the old man. *Abu Harry*, Harry's father, sat at the kitchen table, scribbling his thoughts on scraps of paper, murmuring to himself.

"I had a dream, *octee*, my sister," Shaima said as she dipped a brush into the bowl, painting the oily mixture on top of the newly kneaded pita-sized dough discs.

"What was your dream about, sister?" she asked.

Shaima nodded towards *Abu Harry* and lowered her voice. "*Baadayn*, later. Tell you after our meal. We don't want to get him all worked up again."

"*Masboot*, you're right."

The last thing anyone wanted was for the *mashnoon* crazy old man to become unraveled again. The last time it took both of them hours to calm him when he woke up from a terrible nightmare. He pulled his hair and cried out about the visions he saw at the mount of Megiddo. They had promised Harry they would do their best to care for his father, but this was turning into a hopeless feat. Appeasing him by appealing to his ego, asking him questions about time travel or other related theories, was a solution which usually worked, but as the days went by, even this had little effect. Fortunately, a pot of boiled *babuhnij*, chamomile tea, managed to settle him down. Sometimes they added a dose of crushed sleeping pills into the drink.

"All right, sister. I am going back to my mending in the salon. I'll let you finish up here," she said signalling with her eyes for Shaima to come join her.

"I will finish baking and come sit with you when they're done cooling," Shaima replied, giving her a wink.

Nazreen washed her hands and dried them on the dish towel hanging on the fridge door handle. She tossed her apron over the kitchen chair and walked past Harry's father towards the salon.

Flashbacks crept into Nazreen's mind remembering things before the battle at the mount of Megiddo. *Abu Harry,* Harry's father, had insisted they remain inside at all times. Shaima demanded to know who would feed the goats and chickens, tend to the garden and gather eggs from the coop. After all, they still had to eat. His initial concerns were addressed when they agreed he would accompany them outside as needed.

It was all for nothing. Soon after, *Abu Harry* fell into his own world, immersed in his conversations with the invisible people, barely noticing the sisters' presence. When it came time to go outside, Shaima and Nazreen ventured out together justifying to themselves this old man couldn't protect them even if he wanted to.

The wind whistled through the hallway.

Had someone forgotten to shut the front door again?

"*Nazreen. Octee, sister. Ta-allee! Come here!*" a young girl called out to her.

It can't be, she thought to herself. She hurried down the hall.

The door was not open as she'd first thought. *How did the wind come into the house?* She turned the knob, pushed the door open and stepped out onto the veranda. Lightning streaks lit up the scorched sky while dark clouds pregnant with fire rolled turbulently towards the south (towards Jerusalem *Abu Harry* had speculated earlier.) These events of nature resulted from the battle to end all battles happening at the mount of Megiddo.

She closed her eyes as the howling of the winds filled her ears and pulled at her clothes. Her long hair whipped over her shoulders like the pink tassels on the handles of her little sister's bicycle. The tears she had been fighting back burned her cheeks. In her vision, she saw her little sister Nosayba waving to her. It was how she remembered seeing her darling sweet sister the last time they were together. It was the day when Nosayba had faded into a radiant light right before their eyes.

CHAPTER 33
WHERE ALL WORLDS CROSS

From Cristal's quick assessment of her surroundings, the dark and cramped space signalled they had landed inside another closet. Raffe turned to her, his elbow grazing her arm.

"The closets are either getting smaller or you're going to have to cut down on those chocolate-filled croissants," she whispered.

He cracked a half smile. "Before we head into battle, I will make you the best Nutella *babka* in the world."

Which of the worlds was he referring to? Earth, Limbo or...? She noticed Raffe was dressed in his usual white T-shirt which was one size too small and a pair of skinny black stone washed jeans. Aside from the wings folded on his back, he looked like any ordinary Israeli.

The bracelet vibrated gently against her skin. Waves of energy rippled around her body. Glancing down she realized instead of the GN issued grey garb, her body was now clothed in a silvery white long sleeved tunic with matching leggings. On her feet were silver ankle-high laced boot sandals which resembled *calsei*, first century Roman military boots. The new attire had a life of its own, pulsating a warm energy against her skin.

"What is this?" she asked, pointing to her clothes.

His eyes narrowed while his lips curled into a smirk. "That is your uniform."

"Uniform?"

"A Lieutenant Commander must be dressed accordingly. Do you not approve?"

Her mouth dropped open. "Lieutenant Commander?" She blinked back her astonishment and managed to say, "I'm honored and humbled."

He gave his customary grunt. "Are you done with the questions?"

"One more question."

He crossed his arms over his chest and heaved a sigh.

"If you call this my uniform, what do you call yours?" she asked, nodding to his outfit.

He gave a big laugh which shook the walls of the closet and rattled the items on the shelves. "You don't like it? Would you rather me wear my armor of light instead? Of course, I prefer to only wear that during battle."

"I see," she said with a grin.

He opened his hand towards the door. "Shall we?"

She took in a deep breath, wondering if she should have used her questions to ask him what was behind the door. Her innate stubbornness and pride overrode the practicality of simply asking him. "*Never let anyone know you know less than they do,*" her father once told her.

"Age before beauty," she replied, opening her hand in the same manner.

With one eye-brow raised, he said, "As you wish."

He walked through the door, leaving her behind in the cramped closet.

"Hm," she murmured to herself. "I can do this."

She focused her thoughts on the door.

"Allow me to pass through you," she commanded.

The door melted before her eyes revealing Raffe on the other side. His back was to her and his hand gestures gave the impression he was talking to someone.

She stepped through the door, glancing back to see it return to solid form. She quickly scanned the room. Raffe was talking with a man and a woman. The light streaming from the windows behind them cast silhouettes which hid their identity, but their voices gave them away.

"Dad! Bina!" she cried out.

"Cristal!"

Her father opened his arms and she ran towards him, throwing herself into his embrace.

"Thank God, you're okay!" He buried his face in her hair and held her close to him. Another pair of arms wrapped around her.

"We knew you'd come back," Bina said.

Raffe cleared his throat, interrupting the reunion. She stepped back noticing a dark cloud pass over her father's face while Bina's smile melted into a thin line.

Raffe said, "Ms. Schwartz before you try to pull another impressive escape, I want to inform you both that you no longer need to fear me. Cristal can confirm this if you doubt my intentions."

Cristal flashed them a smile, hoping it was enough to reassure them. "Yes, you can trust Raffe now. He isn't here to capture you guys."

Carlos, her father, raised his brow and tilted his head. "And how do we know he isn't holding you here against your will?"

She looked her dad straight into his eyes and said, "Because I asked God to order Raffe to stop hunting you."

Bina's expression on her face turned from concern into awe. "You spoke with the Almighty God?"

Cristal felt her cheeks turn pink. "Yes I spoke with Him briefly."

Raffe waved his arms, raising his voice. "We have no time to explain all the details. The Almighty has summoned all those in Limbo to join the battle against the false messiah."

Carlos turned to Bina and they exchanged knowing looks.

"We have been watching the battle in the reflection pool. Kerim and the angel forces along with the Resurrected are outnumbered. Bezel and his followers are in the hundreds of thousands," he said.

Bina interrupted him. "All the souls from the GN experiments are ready to fight. From our last count, there are about a couple thousand. Not a large number but we have prepared them with spiritual warfare training."

Carlos continued. "We will still be vastly outnumbered and..."

"We must have faith in God," Cristal said with conviction.

Carlos gave her a gentle smile and said, "Cristal, I wasn't finished yet."

Raffe snorted back a laugh. "Your daughter is very eager to lead."

"Of course, please finish, Dad," she said, throwing Raffe a look.

Bina touched Carlos' hand and he nodded for her to continue. "We recruited souls here in Limbo. They number to a bit over half a million. We've done what we could to prepare them for the battle in the short amount of time we were working with."

Raffe said, "You have done well. It is time."

Carlos sucked in his breath, gave Cristal a reassuring look and said to Bina, "We've been waiting for this moment. Give them the order now."

Without hesitation, she clapped her hands, the sound causing the ground to shake beneath their feet. Soon after, rhythmic footsteps marching in unison filled their ears.

"What is that?" Cristal asked.

"The souls are headed to the hill of Megiddo where all worlds cross. We await your orders," Bina replied.

CHAPTER 34
THE BATTLE

Vulture-like demons, bald headed with large hooked bills and six-foot wing spans, circled above waiting to swoop down on the fallen. Today marked the first one hundred days from the Day of the Third Trumpet. The sky was an angry blood red filled with ferocious lightning clouds crackling with spiritual energy.

Harry and Serena spent the precious few hours they had together reflecting on all that had happened. They recalled the day they'd first arrived at Mount Megiddo when they realized the *mount* was actually a hill.

"The movies always made it seem Armageddon would be more terrifying," Serena said to Harry that day.

Upon arriving to the mount, the angels announced God had declared Kerim as the commander for the upcoming battle. It was ironic how only a few years back in a different time and place, Harry had been the one to give Kerim orders.

"I realize how tiny we are in the grand scheme of things," he told Serena.

"Yes, everything we've encountered before this seems inconsequential," she replied.

Kerim commanded the motley crew of angelic, resurrected and human recruits to prepare for war, assigning everyone into groups with specific duties based on their skills and expertise. The mayor of the village was assigned to hand out desert camouflage uniforms, consisting of a jacket, trousers, T-shirt and brown combat boots.

The mayor of the village told them, *"Abu Walid* and the angels instructed us to prepare for the battle."

Walid's eyes narrowed upon hearing this. His father's secrets were still difficult to accept.

"We've been collecting military gear and equipment for decades," the mayor continued. "We never questioned where or how he obtained the equipment. As instructed, we built several underground armories and shelters to hold them."

Harry and Walid were ordered to accompany a few angels and resurrected recruits to return to the village to gather ground equipment, rocket and grenade launchers and air defence shoulder-launch surface-to-air missiles. From the list, the most impressive military equipment in the stash was the Israeli Iron Dome, a mobile all-weather air defence system made up of four launchers used to intercept incoming missiles.

Walid said, "I remember helping my father store the Iron Dome."

Harry raised his brow. "I've only seen one in a news article. Didn't you wonder why he had one in his possession?"

Walid shrugged. "He was a man of few words. Don't

forget, he was a general in the Israeli Army. I never questioned him."

When Walid's mother told stories of her past, it dawned on Harry that General Assaf was in fact Walid's father. On one of their trips back from the village Harry mentioned this to Walid. They'd been driving back additional equipment; computer servers, solar panels, and generators. Harry was in charge of setting up a network at the camp to connect with available Truth Seeker contacts. In the past few weeks, the number of Truth Seekers communicating on his *interranet* had dwindled from hundreds of thousands to only a few hundred.

Walid was driving when Harry said, "I met your father when Serena and I first arrived in Megiddo."

"*Anjiad?* You did?" Walid glanced over at him.

"Yeah, he was the one who helped free Cristal from GN Tel Aviv. We suspect he moved the other patients to save them from GN's soul separation program. Your father is a true hero. He sacrificed a lot."

"*Inshallah*, God willing, he will know how much I love and respect him," Walid said.

"As they say, God moves in mysterious ways. Have faith in Him."

Walid gave him a wry grin. "Yes, we must have faith."

THE VILLAGERS CALLED IT A MIRACLE. THE TOP OF THE HILL where they'd set up their military base and headquarters began to grow. Serena noticed vehicles were taking longer to travel to and from the village. Harry, busy with his duties, didn't put much thought to her observations.

A week later, the base of the hill began swelling and erupting like a horrible boil lifting and stretching the top of the hill until it became a vast plateau. Harry and Serena drove to the north side and saw the once soft slope of the hill was now a steep drop-off. The valley below stretched for miles in all directions.

"A miracle! A miracle!" Villagers collapsed on the ground.

"Praise Almighty God," *Im Walid* cried out. "Pray for His Mercy."

Three times a day, *Im Walid* fell to her knees, looked to the heavens with her open palms raised and prayed. It signalled others to pray and they did so in the ways they were taught.

Not having been brought up in religious homes, Harry and Serena felt awkward.

"What's the right way to pray?" Serena whispered to Harry.

Kerim, who had been overseeing the strategic planning with a small group of angels, overheard their conversation and came over to where they stood.

Harry said, "With all the spiritual warfare training, we learned how to pray to invoke or to defend. But we never learned how to just pray to God."

"There is no wrong or right way to pray," Kerim said. "Ask God to help guide you. Remember that when you pray, it has to be genuine and come from your heart."

Kerim gave a nod and left.

From that day forward, Harry spent quiet moments on his knees with his eyes closed. He prayed,

Dear God, I'm not sure how to do this and so I ask for Your help and guidance. I haven't been a holy kind of guy. But I pray you forgive me for my shortcomings. Thank you for giving myself and

Serena the honor to be in your army. We ask you to give us the wisdom and strength and your Holy Spirit to do Your Will.

Harry found solace when Serena held his hand and prayed silently with him.

Later that same day, Kerim ordered Serena and a few of the Resurrected to map out their new geographical landscape.

Serena reported back that the sheer sides of the mountain were daunting for even a skilled mountain climber like herself.

"Doable but only for the experienced and well-equipped," she said.

The plateau of the mountain which had been the top of the hill was the size of approximately five football fields. Descending to the valley required physical strength and climbing expertise which only a few had, leaving most of the villagers stranded at the top. For this reason, Harry, Serena, Walid and the angels were assigned to continue gathering supplies and equipment from the village.

Grumbling erupted among the resurrected villagers. They began praying to God asking He provide a way for them to return to their homes. Many wanted to check on children they left behind or to gather more food and supplies. "A supernatural elevator, perhaps?" a few asked.

When Kerim got wind of this, he blew up. "Stop asking God for material things or access to them. We are about to battle the anti-christ. We are not on a camping trip!"

The complaints ceased soon after Serena reported the first sighting of GN troops moving in from the far north.

"Global Nation Russian troops have entered Afula city in the Jezreel valley. Some on foot, some in army vehicles and some just 'appeared.' Reports from the Truth Seekers' interranet from local sources in Metula, a town on the border of Lebanon followed by those in Akko and Haifa have corroborated our findings," she said.

Kerim gazed over the valley, saying in a low voice, "So it won't be a pure spiritual war after all. This could be a ruse, but we will play by human warfare rules for now."

Harry provided his update. "The Truth Seekers who remain in their towns are risking their lives to provide us with intel. Many residents in the area have either died, gone missing or are heading en masse to the south. The GN Russian troops have gone through each city and village, rounding up people to join them or face death. They await your orders."

Kerim looked far into the distance as he spoke. "Their self-sacrifice has given them a place in Heaven. Tell them the Almighty God will be with them on Judgment Day. Their order is to stay low and remain where they are until further notice."

Russian-led GN troops, mainly from Russia and Iran and a consortium of smaller Eastern European countries, claimed a part of the valley several hundred miles from the base of the mount of Megiddo. They set up tents and shelters digging in for what could be a prolonged war. On makeshift flag poles, they raised Russian and Iranian GN flags. The flags flapped wildly in the wind, declaring their defiance against God.

"From our estimates, there are a few thousand troops but more are arriving daily. I'll have an assessment report on their artillery fire power shortly. GN Tel Aviv troops have not been sighted yet, but our contacts in Tel Aviv say they are preparing," Serena reported back.

The angels had their own meetings when the Resurrected

were out of hearing range. They often discussed with each other about the impending arrival of Bezel and other spiritual warfare matters. Harry and Serena listened, trying to absorb the information which often was way above their heads.

Several of the villagers said, "Maybe we won't be fighting after all. How can GN troops climb the steep sides of the mountain God has created?"

"GN has jets and drones. Why do they come with ground troops?" others asked.

"Rumor has it God grounded all aircraft since the earthquake."

"We heard that it is the president of Israel and Global Nation, the anti-christ, that has grounded all aircraft."

Harry and Serena chose not to add to the gossip, but they knew demons were unable to teleport outside of the country since Bezel became the president of Israel and Global Nation, technically the self-appointed leader of the world.

Kerim remained stoic and resolute during this period. Harry and Serena were to advise the villagers to stop their speculation and focus on the mission at hand.

These were things Harry noted in his online blog on the Truth Seekers' interranet network. He needed to reassure his followers to have faith in God. He felt it also his duty to record all that was happening for the sake of future generations.

Serena asked, "If everything you've written sits on the Truth Seekers' cloud interranet servers, what will happen if all digital technology and access to it are destroyed? Shouldn't you print your writing and bury it somewhere for someone to dig up in the future?"

"Got that covered. The beauty of technology is I've got

3D printers attached to all the servers. They are set to automatically print each page daily and compile into a 3D book once it hits three hundred and fifty pages. The pages of the book are made from a fire resistant carbon geopolymer created at GN New York labs. We call it steel stone paper, an indestructible pliable lightweight material originally designed for light weight armor."

Her jaw dropped. "And when were you going to tell me about this?"

He coughed into his hand, holding back a chuckle. "Walid and I brought back a 3D printer from the village. I was going to surprise you with books 1 and 2 after I finish writing book 3 which as you can see, the story is still unfolding."

She rolled her eyes and folded her arms on her chest. "How convenient."

Harry went to his duffel bag and dug out the two books. They were each the size of a regular 6x9 inch paperback although slightly thicker due to each page being twice the thickness of regular paper. He handed them to her.

She examined the books in silence, maintaining the pout on her face. After a few moments, curiosity overcame her. "They almost look like your everyday paperback except the print is engraved into the pages. And I noticed you have braille embossing underneath each line. I love it!"

"Read inside the cover," he said.

She flipped to the page after the cover and saw Harry's handwritten note.

For my dear Serena, my wife, my love and best friend.

She closed the book, a hint of a tear gleamed in her eye. Still holding the books, she wrapped her arms around him.

"Did I ever tell you how much I love you?" she asked.

He pulled her close, holding her tightly. "I love you too. Never forget that," he said, kissing the top of her head.

LATER THAT NIGHT THE EVENTS OF THE DAY TRIGGERED HIS inner unrest. At that moment, his mother's voice entered his mind, consoling him with her words of wisdom. No longer under GN's surveillance, he freely communicated with her telepathically. Being able to contact her in the 'other' Megiddo was comforting.

"*Ma, it's been a tough day,*" he said in his head.

"*Be strong, Harrell,*" she responded. "*We are with you. God is with you.*"

On this particular night, she read from the Jewish Bible, the Book of Proverbs. He closed his eyes allowing the words to resonate through him.

"When your fear comes like a storm, and your calamity comes like a whirlwind; when trouble and straits come upon you

Because they hated knowledge, and did not choose the fear of the Lord;

they did not desire my advice, they despised all my reproof;

they will eat of the fruit of their way, and from their counsels they will be sated,

for the backsliding of the naive shall slay them, and the tranquility of the fools shall cause them to perish.

Then they will call me, and I will not answer; they shall seek me, and they shall not find me.

But he who hearkens to me shall dwell confidently and shall be tranquil from the fear of harm."

—*Book of Proverbs Chapter 1, Torah, translation by Rabbi A.J. Rosenberg*

HARRY HELD SERENA CLOSE TO HIM AS THEY LAY INSIDE their sleeping bag in the tent which they shared with Walid and his mother. The small luxuries they had taken for granted for most of their lives such as showering, eating a warm meal and sleeping in a bed seemed like distant memories. He watched Serena's eyes dart back and forth under her eyelids. Even in her sleep, she was gathering intelligence and planning strategic missions.

It was one of the rare nights Harry and Serena had the same rotating shift. He kissed her on the forehead and tried to drift off himself. He needed all the energy he could get.

THE GN FORCES GREW IN NUMBER OVER THE FOLLOWING days. Artillery fire rained down on the perimeters of the north side of the mountain. A task force of GN soldiers had begun scaling up the mountain side.

"At the pace they're going, they'll reach the plateau by morning," Serena said. Although the mountain had steep sides, it only stood 7700 feet.

Walid and his mother were on the north side with other resurrected villagers hurling rocks down the mountain side. Kerim had said as long as GN did not use spiritual warfare, angels were to refrain from using their angelic powers. They were not to use spiritual force unless given the order.

Gusts of one hundred mile an hour winds began blasting through the valley, tearing down the tents and ripping apart the GN camp. The blustery columns of wind continued their path towards the Mount of Megiddo, crashing against the side, plunging GN soldiers hanging onto the crags of the mountainside to their bloody deaths. Mangled bodies littered the base of the mount as the winged demons swooped down to collect their spoils. The winds howled and whimpered like a pack of she-wolves in labor.

"Another miracle!" the villagers cried out. But the celebration was short-lived.

GN forces began launching missiles from the eastern side, taking the villagers by surprise despite Kerim's warnings to continue being vigilant. One missile hit a small stockpile of ammunition, killing those in close range, one being the mayor's wife.

"Have mercy on us, dear Lord God!" the mayor cried out with his wife's body in his arms.

The shrieking sounds of missiles flying through the air and blasts nearby caused others to run for cover. Those whose loved ones were killed by the missile remained unfazed.

Kerim said, "The battle is not going to wait. Get back to your positions!"

A shell whistled overhead landing several feet from where they stood.

"*Haram*. This is forbidden! We must bury our dead. We cannot fight and leave their bodies here," *Im Walid* said firmly.

The small group cried out in agreement. "We'd rather die!"

Kerim gave a swift nod. "*Im Walid*, you will need to coordinate quickly. You and the others must return to your positions once the mission is done. Walid and Harry will give you cover."

Preparations were made for the burials despite the chaos. The winged demons circled above thirsting for the souls of the recently fallen.

Harry felt Serena's presence beside him. "They need me at the front lines," she said in a soft voice.

He ached to hold and protect her from the horrors. "Keep yourself safe. I'll be praying for you," he said, turning to her.

Strands of hair like golden wheat peeked out from under her helmet, her pale blue eyes locking her gaze with his. "More blood will be spilled today. Pray that God gives us the will to do what needs to be done and spare as many as we can, especially those souls who are lost but still can be saved," she said.

"And pray that He grants us the wisdom to know the difference," he replied. "Stay safe."

"I'll be fine, Harry." Tilting her face up, she pressed her lips against his.

He closed his eyes, relishing the fleeting moment of intimacy between them. She pulled away, breaking the spell, his wishful attempt at suspending time.

"We'll get through this, ok? I'll be back in no time," she said. He traced the side of her cheek with his hand. The knot in his chest swelled with anguish.

"Yeah, take care of yourself" was all he could manage to say.

Placing his hand in hers, she turned it over and kissed the palm with her petal soft lips. Wordless goodbyes.

He watched her walk away, the setting sun glowing around

her. He fought back the desire to go after her. *I should be protecting her, not sending her out on a suicide mission.*

Had he not been assigned to stay back, he would have joined the covert offensive operation to infiltrate and penetrate GN assault regiments on the ground. GN forces grossly outnumbered and outgunned theirs. Except for the angels, the chances of the rest of the task force returning intact were slim.

"Dear God, I put my faith and trust in You. Please help bring her back safely," he said under his breath.

CHAPTER 35
ANGELS AT BATTLE OF MEGIDDO

The following course of events happened swiftly as if each day was only half. The morning after Serena had left for the covert operation on the battlefield, Harry was jostled awake by *Im Walid*.

"You must come with me! *Yallah*! Hurry, let's go!" she cried.

He stumbled out of the tent into the darkness. The smell of death was in the air and a small group of villagers were gathered at the entrance of the camp with several pointing towards the skyline.

"What's going on?" he asked. *Was Serena okay?*

Im Walid waved for him to follow her. She dashed ahead joining the group. Harry's heart pounded in his chest as he chased after her.

"It is happening!" he heard someone say.

"Look!" another cried out.

What was happening?

Serena and the task force were supposed to be back before sunrise. He scoured the crowd but didn't spot her. Walid and his mother were looking westward in the same direction as the others. He turned his gaze and saw the cause of the commotion. Just above the horizon, a blood orange sun was rising from the west.

THE NEXT EVENT HAPPENED LATER THAT MORNING. FROM the north, south and east of Mount Megiddo, GN troops began gathering.

"We're surrounded!" an older woman cried.

Harry and Walid were assigned to a special task force ready to scale down the west side of the mountain. They estimated it would take them at least half a day. When they reached the base of the mountain their digital clocks indicated only ten minutes had passed.

"Ten minutes? Am I reading that right?" Walid asked.

The archangel called Selaphiel said, "Where the spiritual and mortal worlds cross is where we stand. Human time is a blink of an eye in Heaven."

The angel-speak was often puzzling and difficult to comprehend. The human brain's limitations meant human beings would never fully grasp the complexities of the spiritual realm and beyond. On the opposite spectrum, spiritual beings found human beings perplexing and difficult to communicate with or understand. Even angels who dwelled on Earth in human form found it difficult to relate or communicate with humans despite being able to technically speak any language. Harry had resolved not to question his angelic superiors even if it meant not fully comprehending what was said. In this instance, he wondered to himself if the speeding up of human time was affecting their enemy in the same way or not.

Intel was coming in through their headsets that the troops were settling around newly created camps.

"From our assessment, the troops are mainly made up of humans with possibly a few hundred demons," an angel keeping watch informed them.

To the human eye, low-level demons appeared to be human-like in appearance. Angels, however, were able to see past their facade. Being that the other five of the task force were archangels, Harry and Walid relied on their expertise.

The fiercest looking archangel called Azrael said, "Fear not. The mortal soldiers are not well trained. I smell their fear. Their numbers are meaningless."

Walid with an M16 in his hands, elbowed Harry on the arm. "Azrael is the Angel of Death," he said under his breath. "He would know if Lioness is okay or not."

Hearing Serena's code name 'Lioness' pained Harry's heart, though he tried to ignore it.

Walid cracked a lopsided smile. "We're surrounded by archangels and so is she. We're as safe as we can possibly be."

The sky was a dark purple with the sun hanging above them like a blazing orange red mandarin. Overshadowed but still visible, the moon, worn and faded, stared at them with sorrowful eyes, a jagged scar zigzagging down the middle of its face.

Walid sucked in his breath. *"Ya Allah!* Oh my God! The moon has split."

"Not doubting you but could it be an optical illusion?" Harry asked.

"No, it is real. It is another sign," he replied firmly.

Harry was about to ask more when they were interrupted.

"We're hearing chatter. We have eyes on Lioness. 32°34'30.2" N 35°10'46.9" E," came over their headsets.

Harry took note of the coordinates displayed on his high tech ballistic eyewear. "She's on the south side."

They made their way to the south of the mountain, hiding behind boulders. About five miles out, with their binoculars, they spotted one of the angels from the task force.

Azrael was the first to comment. "Appears they've blended in with GN troops."

"So they've succeeded in infiltrating the enemy?" Walid asked.

"They've gone dark. We need a volunteer to see if they need extraction," he said.

Archangel Mikail, aka Archangel Michael, had the same fearsome qualities of Azrael but was an angel of few words. In contrast to Azrael's stone black eyes, raven black hair and ruddy complexion, Mikail's eyes were an almost colorless silver, his hair like a cap of snow, blending into his pearly skin. Archangel Mikail's reputation as a warrior preceded him. Earlier briefings revealed Mikail's rank was equivalent to the General of the Armies and that he was the one mentioned in the Bible as the archangel who battled Satan.

"I will go," Mikail said. His angelic voice, human masked but filled with a celestial bass vibrato, sent a shiver up Harry's spine.

Harry asked Walid under his breath, "Shouldn't someone of his rank send another to go in his place?"

The question caused the Angel of Death's head to turn.

"The way of the angels are very different from those of man," Azrael growled. "It is Humans who allow the lowest rank to fight the battles while those of higher rank command from afar."

Harry and Walid exchanged looks remembering, even in human form, angels had extraordinary heightened senses.

THE NIGHT TURNED INTO DAY AND RETURNED JUST AS swiftly. Thousands of GN troops began arriving. Harry and Walid along with the angels changed into GN combat uniforms. They moved into the GN camp when night fell.

They spotted Serena with a few female soldiers sitting in a tent filled with communication equipment and monitors.

Mikail had connected with the other angels from the first task force. He confirmed Serena would be sending out intel to them soon.

"Lioness has confirmed there are Truth Seekers and rebels embedded with the troops," Mikail said when they returned to the base of the mountain. "There is an operation in motion to destroy the bulk of GN artillery. This has to happen before sunrise."

Azrael asked, "Before sunrise? Why?"

Mikail lowered his voice. "Bezel will be here by morning, GN troops plan to attack our troops full scale."

Harry felt his pulse race. Walid turned to him, his eyes wide with fright.

Mikail directed his icy stare towards them. "Do not fear. This has been as it has been intended all along."

Walid's voice shook. "Shouldn't we assist in the operation to destroy the artillery?"

The archangel's face remained expressionless as a statue. "General Assaf is overseeing the mission."

He replied, "My father is here?" He glanced over at Harry.

Mikail gave the usual grunt and turned away, his tolerance for human banter waning.

The sun was setting in the east just then. A cloud of black fog rolled into the sky like volcanic smoke. When the fog reached them, the winged demons circling above came hurtling to the ground landing at the feet of Mikail and Azrael.

Mikael's lips curled into a menacing smile. "Is it time?" he asked Azrael.

Azrael closed his eyes for a moment as if listening for instruction. "The Almighty says to do what must be done in His name."

Mikail's silvery hair whipped across his face as the winds began picking up around them. From his back, he pulled out a long fire-hilted sword and raised it above his head releasing a burst of energy which radiated across the valley. Letting out an unearthly roar, he cried, "In the name of the Almighty YHWH, the one true God, begone from here and return to the wretchedness of hell!" The sword fell into the vile mass causing an explosion felt for thousands of miles, obliterating the winged demons from the Earth.

All those who witnessed this trembled in fear.

LATER THAT NIGHT, HARRY LOGGED ONTO THE TRUTH

Seeker interranet from his cell phone and posted what he witnessed on the Truth Seeker blog. He had recorded the event with his camera, but when he tried to play back the video, all that was captured was Walid staring at an empty space where the angels stood.

CHAPTER 36
PLACE WHERE BOTH WORLDS CROSS

Cristal gazed over the valley below the mount of Megiddo where the recruited soldiers of Limbo were awaiting battle. On this side of the parallel worlds, the breeze drifted across the valley gently brushing the tops of the green and red vegetation. The sun peeked out from behind pillows of white clouds and she basked under its gentle rays.

Meanwhile, her father and Bina were discussing a defensive strategy called Deep Defense.

"It worked for the Germans in WWI," Carlos insisted. "We keep the GN battalions at bay. Push them further back from the base of the mount."

Bina sighed. "That would work if supernatural warfare was not at play."

He said, "From what we can see, the battle has shown zero signs of supernatural offensives. Having multiple defence lines will slow them down and allow our human and soul troops to rotate out safely at the top of the mount giving them time to replenish and recover."

Raffe was standing with a group of angel forces presumably doing strategic planning of their own.

Eager to cross over to where her friends were, she tapped into her supernatural ability to view the events unfolding on the "earthly side." She witnessed Serena and the rebel forces infiltrating GN military. GN troops were mainly made up of civilian recruits with little experience in warfare. Dispersed among them were demon possessed soldiers who appeared human-like. Like the angels, Cristal could see past their human persona down to their oil slick form and blood red eyes.

Her attention was drawn towards the top of the mountain where she sensed Kerim's presence. Dressed in army gear, she saw him in the HQ tent giving commands to troops over his headset. Several times, he sensed her watching and met her gaze.

"*We have to focus on the battle,*" he said in his thoughts.

She blushed. "*Of course. That is all I've been thinking of.*"

Traces of a smirk crossed his lips.

"*The archangels are fascinated by the human who accomplished what no one has.*"

"*Oh? And what was that?*"

"*Closing down Purgatory.*"

She gave a snort. "*Is that how they're going to write it down in history books?*"

"*It is how they see it, so be it.*"

"*You're beginning to sound like an angel.*"

"*Isn't that what I am?*"

"*Of course.*" She gave a short sigh.

"What's really bothering you? I can feel your anxiety. And don't say it's nothing. Spit it out and let's deal with it fast. The war isn't going to wait and many lives are at stake."

His blunt observation stung but she needed the slap of reality. What kind of a warrior was she when the next mission went against all her values? "I can't imagine killing another human being," she admitted.

Kerim's tone grew serious. *"If it is the will of the Almighty, so be it. Trust in Him."*

"I don't know if I can commit murder even if it is in the name of God."

He softened his tone, knowing too well human emotions were hard to overcome, even for an angel. *"Do not allow your human emotions blind you. You are the instrument of the Lord. Remember that."*

His words left her feeling more unsettled.

In the background, she could hear someone call out to Kerim.

"I must go," he said. *"Remember, I am always with you. See you on the battleground."*

"Cristal, did you hear what I said?"

She turned to see Bina and her dad's puzzled looks.

"Will you inform Raffe? The troops are ready to cross over," Bina said.

Her silence was met with exasperation. "There are a lot of souls here who are counting on you. Reports that time has sped up on Earth have already been verified. We need to move in now," her dad said, trying to keep his voice calm.

She nodded. "You're right. Every second counts. Fill me in and I'll bring it forward to Raffe."

As she awaited their instructions, she felt someone behind

her and whirled around. Outfitted in GN beige army fatigues stood Joanna Chan, her former arch-nemesis and rival. Her appearance had changed drastically from the last time they saw each other. Her usual coiffured hair was pulled back in a limp ponytail and her face was make-up free.

Joanna gave her a salute and said, "Lieutenant Commander, General Raffe requests for you to join him." Her expression was grim and Cristal sensed her fear.

"Joanna, it's just me," Cristal said. "You don't have to salute here. This isn't Global Nation."

She snapped her eyes forward and stood at attention. "Yes, sir," she said.

With the end of the world at hand, the grudges between them seemed trivial.

"You can drop the military lingo and call me by name," she said.

"Yes, sir," Joanna said, her voice wavering. "I mean, yes, Cristal."

"When did you arrive here?" she asked, softening her tone.

Tears slid down Joanna's face yet she remained at attention. "I'm not exactly sure. The last thing I remember was following Kerim's orders to gather the Resistance out of GN New York campus to the safe zone. The mission was a failure." She stared ahead, reliving the moments before the invasion.

"Go on," Cristal said.

She blinked back the tears and continued. "I woke up here a day or so later. Others like me didn't know what happened or how we got here. In fact it took us days to figure out where here was. Then out of the blue, my dad showed up. As you know, I'd been searching for him for years. He couldn't tell me much just that he was so happy to see me. He brought me to Bina and Carlos."

Cristal shot her dad a look. Didn't Joanna know she was dead? Her father cast his eyes down and shook his head.

"It is time," Bina said. "All will be revealed soon."

SOMETHING WENT TERRIBLY WRONG. THE MISSION TO destroy GN's artillery had failed and those helping Serena were caught. Demon soldiers brought the Truth Seekers resistance fighters in for interrogation. Serena and the angels retreated back to the top of the mountain.

The executions began shortly after. The prisoners were brought out and lined up at the frontline.

"They want us to watch. Those bastards," Serena said, peering through her binoculars.

Suddenly Im Walid wailed, her scream echoing across the valley.

In the lineup General Assaf, her husband, stood tall, his jaw stern and his arms straight at his sides.

Walid was proud to be his son. He drew his mother into his arms, holding her close as she wept. There was nothing to fear for the Almighty God was here with them.

"Do not cry, *Immee*. We will join him very soon in Heaven," he said.

One of the higher ranking GN demon soldiers commanded the human soldiers to point their rifles and shoot.

Harry's gut wrenched at the sight. General Assaf and the

Truth Seekers were facing the death squad and there was nothing he could do about it.

Walid cried out, "Dear God, save their souls!"

Im Walid and the others repeated the cry.

Shots rang out and General Assaf and the others fell to the ground. Harry froze while the fury inside him ignited his spiritual energy causing tremors below their feet. Unleashing this energy could decimate everyone on the ground if he willed it.

"Stand down," Kerim said. "We cannot start a spiritual war without the Almighty's order."

Serena grabbed his hand. "He's right. The demons want us to give in to our emotions."

Suddenly the sound of footsteps marching filled their ears. He sensed hundreds of thousands approaching them from all directions. GN soldiers on the ground began dispersing and running for cover. Even from their vantage point, Harry could not see who or what was coming.

Mikail said under his breath, "Raffe has finally arrived."

Serena clutched his hand tighter. "I see them," she whispered.

In the distance, hundreds of thousands of troops appeared out of thin air from the north, west, east and south, surrounding the GN soldiers. Leading them was a young soldier who marched with a sense of fearlessness, like nothing was going to get in her way.

"Cristal," he gasped.

She was like a silver fiery sword, a bright white light radiating from her core. Raffe marched alongside her, white and blue energy blasting around him. Beside them were a man and woman, glowing in unison with energy pulsating in outward waves.

"Mom," he said softly when he recognized her.

Serena's attention focused on a couple a few rows behind. "I see my mom and dad!" she yelled, pointing towards them. Her heart swelled with mixed emotions. It seemed like forever since they'd been separated. To know they were about to face a bloody war dampened her joy seeing them again.

Sounds of automatic weapons and artillery blasts filled the air.

"To the battle!" Mikail cried.

Harry, Serena, Walid and those assigned to the frontline began descending the mountain.

❧

CRISTAL HAD BLOOD ON HER HANDS. THE SUPERNATURAL battle at Armageddon lasted seven days, but for those who survived, it felt like several weeks.

GN Tel Aviv troops arrived at the battlefield with flags raised.

Archangel Azrael announced, "Bezel is here."

Cristal had sensed his presence long before and wondered if she would see him again face to face.

Much to everyone's surprise, Bezel did not make an appearance and hid inside his tent, away from the fighting.

"Maybe he knows what he's up against," Raffe said when she asked why.

Her ability to see into the minds of the GN soldiers, many not much older than her, made her realize how many truly believed in what they were fighting for.

Like the other holy warriors of the Almighty God, Cristal was obligated to give a warning to GN soldiers before engaging them in battle.

She cried out, "Your leader is the beast from hell. Surrender to YHWH, the one true God Almighty and save your soul!"

"We serve our leader who will reign on Earth as it says in our holy books!" said some.

Others shook with fear saying, "How can you promise to save us? Don't you know what he can do?"

While many more were possessed by demons where no amount of prayers or intervention could save them.

Cristal observed herself from outside her body by detaching her mind from her actions. It was the only way she could deal with the horrors caused by her own hands. She could not overcome the putrid stench from those slain, left baking under the merciless sun. And still they came. Thousands more would replace the slaughtered and more would die by her sword. The air grew heavy with the rotten thickness of death and dying.

And yet out of the thousands, only a small number fell on their knees and asked to be saved. During one such occasion, she found herself confronted by two female GN soldiers cowering before her.

With her sword raised, Cristal cried out, "Surrender to the Almighty God!"

She sucked in her breath.

With their muddied faces and terror-filled eyes, she could barely recognize them. With heads bowed, her former GN guards were begging for their lives. The short one with the baby face, Noa and the tall grumpy Simcha pleaded, "Please save our souls! Save us from our sins. We surrender to the one true God Almighty!"

She recalled during her incarceration at GN the times she had listened to their stories, laughed at their jokes and enjoyed their company despite the circumstances that brought them together. Their small acts of compassion when she was their prisoner flooded her memory.

She cried out, "Do you not remember who I am?"

Noa looked up, trembling with trepidation. "I do not know who you are," she said lifting her arm as if expecting a blow.

Cristal pointed her sword at the tall Simcha. "How about you? Do you know who I am?"

Simcha raised her eyes, grimy tears smeared over her cheeks. She squinted and shook her head. "No, I do not. But I believe you are a messenger of God. Save us, we beg you!"

It was her turn to show compassion.

Raffe had instructed her to recite a prayer for the repentant which she deemed appropriate as she prayed over them.

"God of all Creation, Be with us now and at the hour of our death. Shelter us from harm's way and lead us on the path to eternal life. Receive our life, all that we are, and everything we do. May the Angel of Mercy stay near us this day and always. Amen."

Noa and Simcha closed their eyes, their expressions relaxing as if hearing God's voice in their ears. A warm light fell on them and she saw the hand of God touch their heads.

"Praise God Almighty!" Noa cried, the fear falling away from her.

"Take my soul, dear Lord God!" Simcha said in a loud

voice, her face reflecting the meaning of her name as it shone with joy.

Raffe tapped Cristal on the shoulder. "We must leave them now."

She stepped away, heaving a sigh, knowing full well what the demons were going to do with them. Demon possessed soldiers seized the repentant guards and dragged them away.

"Dear God, please bless and protect them," she whispered.

Raffe's voice filled her ears. "The Almighty God is with them now. You have done what was asked of you."

Recalling the joy on their faces helped settle the anxiety in her heart.

CRISTAL JOINED HER FRIENDS HARRY AND SERENA TO FIGHT alongside the archangels on the battlefield.

Archangel Mikail announced the Almighty's updated rules of engagement. Those with spiritual abilities could now use their powers against the demons and the demon-possessed at the level of their ability. Mikail ordered Harry, Serena, Bina and her father to concentrate their efforts on the demons while she and the archangels focused on saving human souls and destroying those who refused.

Combat did not end when the sun went down. The shell blasts and the shooting continued into the night. The angels did not need sleep and fought non-stop. The human troops, however needed to reboot.

"Go back to base and get some rest," Archangel Mikail commanded the human troops.

Harry, Serena and Cristal ascended to the top of Mount

Megiddo. They were grateful that Raffe had allowed them to use their supernatural abilities to teleport back to base instead of climbing the mountain.

Wrought with the horror they had fully participated in, the three remained silent as they headed to their tents.

"See you back at 0700 hours," Cristal said to them, her voice barely a whisper.

The dark expression on Harry's face mirrored the anguish in her heart. The things they had done and seen could never be erased. He gave her a tired nod and replied in a voice weak with exhaustion, "Roger that. Good night."

Serena could only stare with eyes haunted by horrid images of bullet-ridden corpses strewn over the blood soaked earth. Her once porcelain complexion turned ashen. Harry placed a protective arm around her and led her to their tent.

Cristal could hear Raffe's words of wisdom in her head. "Evil has befallen those blinded by the allure. They sought the truth but fell for the devil's lies and have made him their savior. It is your duty to destroy them. That is an order."

Cristal exhaled slowly as the emotions she'd shoved down during the battle began resurfacing. The ground beneath her feet trembled while the energy inside her throbbed with anticipation. An unsanctioned supernatural disaster triggered by her unstable emotions would be catastrophic.

"Dear God, please give us the strength and guide us to do Your will. Fill us with Your Holy Spirit and protect us from evil and sin," Cristal prayed fervently as she rushed towards her tent.

The muggy air was filled with the distant sound of artillery fire mixed with hushed conversations from within the tents. As her anxiety level increased, her ability to understand all languages weakened. The words muddled together in her head, the volume of the voices getting louder and louder.

"Cristal."

She glanced up and met Kerim's gaze.

"*I need help. I can't do this alone,*" she said in her head.

He reached out and touched her cheek lifting the anxiety from her heart.

"I am always with you," he said.

Overcome with weariness, she collapsed in his arms.

CHAPTER 37
THE RETURN

Before dawn broke, Azrael the Angel of Death, appeared in the sky on a black winged stallion, his dark coal eyes and black armour reflecting the energy radiating from him.

"Bezel has tricked us. Intel has confirmed that he has been hiding in Damascus all along! Angels and those with spiritual powers meet me at the Mount of Olives for The Return!" he cried out.

Cristal rubbed the sleep from her eyes. Everyone had been awakened minutes earlier and were told to gather outside their camp. The sky was eerily dark and an unnerving silence met their ears.

"GN troops have retreated!" someone called out.

They rushed to the north side to see for themselves. Cristal scanned the valley and with her heightened senses confirmed that all human life was destroyed.

Kerim appeared beside her in full angelic form, his silver wings open and ready for flight. "The demons let their human troops battle to their deaths while they left for Syria overnight," he said.

Re-energized by the news, Harry and Serena dressed in the white tunic-style uniforms came and joined them.

"We are ready to go," Harry said.

"Then hurry!" Raffe cried while ascending in the air, his wings spread like an eagle.

Cristal turned to Kerim. "Wish we had wings so we can fly with you," she said.

Harry said, "We can teleport there, just the same."

Kerim gave her a wink. "Give me your hand," he said. She reached out and he pulled her onto his back, his mighty wings flapping, pulling her up into the sky.

He looked over his shoulder and called out, "See you guys there. Harry, make sure to bring Bina, Carlos, Walid and Im Walid."

The breeze brushed against her cheeks as the morning sun began peeking over the western horizon.

"Now hold on tight," he said. "We're about to go Turbo Speed."

JERUSALEM

OUTSIDE THE GARDENS OF GETHSEMANE, Harry and the others sat and waited on the walls of an abandoned outpost facing the Mount of Olives. Gethsemane, once a popular tourist attraction was now one of many makeshift homeless camps. Men and women from all walks of life crammed themselves in any space they could: in the grotto, on the grounds and inside and around the church.

"Harry's father was right. It seems like everyone and their grandmother are in Jerusalem," Walid said.

"I don't understand why," Serena said.

"People have traveled from different continents to witness the fulfillment of their religious prophecies," Bina said.

"We are standing in the place where Jesus' prayed to God the night before he was crucified," Carlos added.

"Oh brother," Harry mumbled.

Serena elbowed him. "What's wrong with you?"

Prior to the earthquake, Christian pilgrims from around the world would come with tour groups just for the opportunity to retrace the steps of Jesus' life all the way up to his crucifixion. Their fascination of reliving the life of someone from centuries ago seemed morbid and purposeless. His Israeli circle of friends had felt the same way.

The Gardens of Gethsemane was enclosed behind an iron fenced wall where giant olive trees, gnarled and stooped with age, fanned their huge branches providing shade for those not acclimated to the Middle Eastern heat. The garden paths once filled with colorful flowerbeds and plants were now overgrown with weeds. Beside the garden, not surprisingly stood a giant basilica, a large Catholic church with huge pillars holding up giant arches at the entrance steps.

"This holy city is where it all happens," Carlos said.

"What do you know about Jerusalem?" Harry asked.

Bina pressed her lips together but held her tongue.

"It is the holiest place on Earth," Carlos replied, raising his brow.

Walid gave Harry a knowing look. "For a place named City of Peace, it is the bloodiest place on Earth," he said.

Im Walid said, "Wars were started and many were killed fighting over this land."

Harry was about to add his own thoughts but was silenced by Serena's glare.

Jerusalem had always been a tinder box ready to explode. Harry and many of his friends avoided the city, exasperated by the tension from the city's inhabitants. Driving the many narrow winding roads congested with giant tour buses and taxis was a challenge even for the most experienced Israeli driver. Honking of car horns was common place with tourists and locals pushing and shoving through the crowded streets, criss-crossing busy roads wherever it suited them, and yelling at anyone who pushed back. In Jerusalem, racism from both sides was the most rampant in all of Israel. Conversations on the street were filled with "those Arabs" or "those Jews," with both sides pointing fingers at the other, unwilling to get along but forced to exist on this small plot of holy land where centuries of spilled blood marked the ground. The world nations would come in with their endless promises but never really wanting a resolution.

Tourists came to Jerusalem with awestruck wonder lured by images of the Golden Dome and the ancient walls of the Old City splashed all over fancy travel websites and postcards. They came to pay pilgrimage to the holy sites and unwittingly empty their pocket books to the local vendors who smirked at their reverence. Unlike the foreigners, Israelis were all too familiar with Jerusalem's dark underbelly, the side where the zealots and the extremists walked a thin line.

"I see them!" Serena said, peering through binoculars.

At the top of the mount which overlooked the city, the archangels stood in what once was an observation point that looked like a mini-amphitheatre with cement seats that wrapped in half circles, and stepped down from the top to the railing overlooking the city. He could see Cristal and Kerim off to the side, having their own intense conversation.

"What exactly are we waiting for?" Serena whispered.

Walid smiled. "For The Return," he said.

"The return? Return of what?"

"Not return of 'what.' The Return of Isa, peace be upon Him," Im Walid said, clasping her hands together.

Serena gave a blank stare. "I am not familiar with all this. What exactly do you mean?"

Harry leaned over and whispered in her ear. "In English, they call him Jesus."

Her eyes widened. "Is that Who we're waiting for?"

A commotion broke out on the streets.

"Look! Look!"

A large group of people were pointing towards the Mount of Olives. Above the mount, the sky opened up and revealed a light so bright it lit up the sky from all corners of the world, blinding ordinary humans who gazed at it.

"I cannot see!" some cried out.

"Dear God! I'm blind!"

Others collapsed on the ground paralyzed by the light.

What followed was the thundering sound of hooves pounding which shook the ground beneath their feet. A voice so pure and strong entered their heads.

"The Son of Man has returned," the Voice said.

Appearing before them on a white winged stallion was the Son of Man, as this was what He wished to be called. His eyes shining a hundred beams of light and fire. Upon His head sat crowns of brilliant stars that twisted and gleamed in every dimension. Those who gazed from the depths of hell weeped and screamed in torment.

Across the world, the remaining survivors felt His presence. The ones who believed in Him were wrapped with a blanket of peace as they awaited their judgment. The people who turned away from the truth, collapsed on the ground, their hearts searching for the warmth of His light but wailed at not finding it.

The Son of Man's armour was coated as if it were dripping in blood, the color of Bordeaux wine. Surrounding Him on white horses and dressed in white uniforms were His Heavenly angelic soldiers ready for battle.

Harry fell on his knees, tears streaking down his cheeks. His heart swelled with the love that radiated from Him. The doubts he had carried all his life were cast away in a single moment. Everyone around him had fallen on the ground with their hands spread upwards to Heaven in supplication.

It was then that the Son of Man waved His hand and immediately a warm sensation, gentle and soothing, fell upon them, healing all who battled in the name of the Almighty God, restoring them to perfect health both physically and mentally. He did not speak aloud for when not in human form, His voice, so powerful and majestic, would kill all mortals who heard it. In their thoughts without a spoken word, He revealed his Heavenly name and the sound of it was so glorious no human name could measure up.

CHAPTER 38
JUDGMENT DAY

Along the winding streets, abandoned buildings and open areas the masses gathered in Jerusalem awaiting their judgment.

Within the walled Gardens of Gethsemane, Dr. Sarah Goldberg knelt on the dry soil with her head and hands pressed to the ground near the roots of an ancient olive tree.

"He is here! He has returned!" she heard them cry.

"Do not look up or you will be blinded by His Divine light," her companions warned her. "We who've not lived holy lives will be judged. We must kneel and pray."

Only half a year ago, Goldberg had risked her life to do what was right. As a self-proclaimed secular Jew, her desire to understand psychosis and the human mind had suppressed her ultra-Orthodox religious upbringing. However, the unethical treatment of patients at GN Tel Aviv caused something inside her to snap. No longer willing to accept the organization's deception nor the strange supernatural occurrences, she yearned to find out the truth behind GN's coma patients.

She had submitted the file about Patient 878 into the GN database against her superior's orders. When a colleague warned of her impending arrest, Goldberg went underground, changing her identity and leaving behind the life she knew. She found the Resistance, people like herself, disillusioned by Global Nation's treatment of citizens, hiding in abandoned buildings.

She joined their movement called Truth Seekers, and they helped her avoid capture by GN forces during nightly raids.

More supernatural incidents surfaced. People were disappearing with witnesses claiming they vanished into thin air. She sought what others were witnessing around the world via the Truth Seeker online blog. Posts about the great earthquake and angels and demons living among them fed her desire to seek the truth. Resisting was no longer enough.

Longing for spiritual guidance and craving the Almighty God's blessing, she traveled on foot to the kibbutz in Megiddo. It was there she heard about the Savior and His return.

With her newfound friends, she made her way to Jerusalem finding the city overflowing with Truth Seekers like her. News of a terrifying battle at Megiddo were discussed in hushed whispers.

She believed these were signs related to the Return of the Messiah and she prayed passionately for God's forgiveness fully comprehending that most of her life she had been blind.

She wondered if she looked up to see the Divine light, maybe now her eyes will be opened. Against her companion's warnings, she raised her head and asked, "Dear Holy Messiah, please forgive me of my sins. I submit my soul to You. Save me from my iniquities."

It was then she heard His Divine Voice. *Your sins are forgiven.*

❦

HARRY LONGED FOR THE MESSIAH TO STAY. HE SHARED THE emotions from everyone around him weeping with joy by His presence.

The Son of Man looked towards the Mount of Olives and seeing the archangels, commanded them to meet at the Gate of Lod.

"We will meet You there!" Mikail cried out.

The Son of Man pulled the reigns and turned His horse towards the north and galloped over top the clouds, the Heavenly army following closely behind.

A violent tremor shook the ground and strong winds swept across the land marking His glorious departure.

Suddenly, everything went black.

❦

CRISTAL STOOD FROZEN, HER GAZE FIXATED TOWARDS THE north, longing to be with Him. Kerim touched her on the shoulder which woke her from her holy reverie, a spiritual trance invoked by His presence.

"Are you okay?" he asked.

"I'm more than okay," she said, her smile stretching from ear to ear. All the fears she once had were washed away.

He chuckled. "Looks like your friends aren't doing so well," he said, pointing over the railing.

She could see them from a distance. They were laying on the ground. At a glance, she wondered if they had passed on but then she saw movement. Harry scratched his nose and turned onto his side, Serena stretched her arms and yawned, and Walid flung his arm above his head.

"Should we wake them?" she asked.

"Let's not. Their souls are rejuvenating. They'll wake up on their own time."

She turned to him. "What will become of us now?"

He took both of her hands in his. "*Ben-Adam,* the Son of Man will kill Bezel and his army with one stroke, by His word alone. This will happen at the airport near Tel Aviv."

She nodded her head. "Ah, yes, the city of Lod. I'm guessing that the Gates of Lod is a historical reference?"

"Very good."

Azrael, Mikail and Raffe were heading towards them.

"Are you going with them?" she asked.

He shook his head. "No, my mission ended at the Battle of Megiddo."

Her heart sank.

Raffe stood beside them and said, "Sorry to interrupt."

She asked, "Will I be joining you?"

Azrael let out a loud chortle, giving Mikail a big slap on the back. Mikail raised his brow but she could see he was holding back a laugh.

"Tell her, Raffe," Azrael said.

Raffe flashed her a rare smile, exposing his popcorn colored teeth. "Your next mission is to accompany Kerim and bring your father and your friends and all the souls from

Limbo and the ones we have saved to the next part of the journey. One way ticket to Heaven. Do not pass Go. Do not collect $200."

She threw her arms around him. "You are the funniest archangel, I've ever met. Thank you Raffe for everything."

Kerim laughed. "I believe Raffe is blushing!"

Raffe shook his head. "No, no. It's just in human form, the sympathetic nervous system floods the skin with blood, hence the color on my cheeks."

Mikail's flared his nostrils. "That doesn't explain why you blush so much as you certainly are not in human form," he said pointing at Raffe's wings.

A trumpet blast interrupted their jovial bantering and the moment of levity transformed into a darker undertone addressing the seriousness of the matter at hand.

"It is time," Azrael said as he began ascending, his wings flapping softly with the breeze.

Mikail, an archangel of few words, was already in flight heading towards Lod.

Raffe patted Kerim on the shoulder. "Take good care of her. She is a special one."

Kerim nodded, giving her a wink. "Of course. I promise to take good care of her."

Raffe spread his wings and flew upwards into the sky, soaring towards Lod.

"What happens with the rest of the people left on Earth?" she asked.

"Not for you to worry any longer, my dear," he said, putting an arm around her.

She looked up at him, recalling the human love she once felt for him.

"What do you mean, once felt? You don't feel it anymore?" he asked with a smirk.

She let out a huge laugh. "I forgot that you can still read my mind."

He hugged her tight. "Before we head to Heaven, tell me how much you still love me in, as you say, 'the human love'."

She blushed three shades of pink. She loved him more than human love. It was a love that transcended time, space and worlds. There was an eternity to spend by his side, serving the Almighty in Heaven. And if after Judgment Day, there was still an earthly world, maybe they could come back together in human form?

"Very good. I never thought of that," he said, kissing the top of her head.

She wrapped her arms around him and a warm light shimmered around them. It seemed an eternity when she was in his arms like this, alone together. What if this never happens again?

"Who said, this may never happen again?" he whispered in her hair.

"Hush," she said. "You're ruining the moment."

He pulled her closer and they held each other quietly as the sky grew a dark angry purple and the rumblings of the ground hinted at the events taking place not far from where they stood. The winds howled and the air grew dense with supernatural energy.

Soon they would be off to lead the others to the next part of the journey.

"Breathe, Cristal, breathe," he said.

"I'm breathing just fine," she said.

CHAPTER 39
EPILOGUE

"**Y***'Allah!* Come on, tell us everything!" Walid's sisters cried out in unison. Dressed in tunics of white light, their joyful glow matched the energy around them.

Abu Walid gazed down at Im Walid with a warm smile. She beamed up at him, her eyes shining with happiness.

They moved over to give space for their sons Walid and Sami to sit. Walid threw Harry a wink and joined in. "*Aywa!* Yes! You must tell us every detail!"

Harry winked back while Serena waved, her infectious smile warming everyone around her. They sat a row behind the Assaf family and beside their own sets of parents. Serena's parents yelled, "Archangel Mikail, tell us!"

Kerim, Cristal and Olivia stood up and joined in the shouts. "Please tell us!"

A few rows away, Gabriel with his parents turned to them and waved. "Tell us!"

Aaron raised his arm and said, "Surely, we deserve to know what happened!"

Sitting beside him, Bina and Carlos chimed in. "We have waited patiently. Please do share!"

The Battle of Lod did not have human witnesses so they were eager to hear the recount of events by the archangels.

At the top of the mount, the archangels were the center of attention. Raffe and Azrael chuckled to themselves as their fellow archangel Mikail inched backwards, shielding himself behind them.

"Oh, no, Mikail! We're not going to steal your limelight," Raffe said, stepping aside, exposing Mikail to the eager audience.

Mikail stared down into the rows and rows of human souls, their faces gleaming with anticipation. Not even the heavenly clouds could hide him now. Struggling to find the words, he cleared his throat.

Azrael leaned over and whispered, "Tell it exactly as it was. In your own words. We have faith in you."

"Yes, I shall do that."

And so he began.

HUMANS WERE UNAWARE THAT THE BEAST HAD A CO-conspirator running Global Nation. We, the archangels, knew of the identity of the second devil. He was the head of Rome and falsely spoke on behalf of the Almighty God.

The Beast and the Roman devil were hiding in Damascus with a small demon army. They thought, surely the GN soldiers would win the battle at Megiddo since they outnumbered the measly group of angels, Resurrected and human soldiers of the Almighty God. Although the mightiest of the Almighty's archangels were in their midst, the Beast believed the numbers were on his side.

During the seven days of the bloodiest battle at Megiddo, the two devils relaxed in the city of Damascus. Not until the final night of battle, when his demon soldiers realized they were no match with the Almighty's army and fled into the darkness of night while leaving their human soldiers to die on the field, did the Beast tremble in fear.

It was then that the Heavens opened up and the Son of Man on his warrior stallion entered the skies of Earth along with His Heavenly army. He was here to destroy the ungodly nations which the Beast ruled upon. He drove the Beast and the head of Rome out of Syria into the Gates of Lod where they were trapped.

The Son of Man opened His mouth and out came a sword, sharpened and ready to take down the Beast's feeble army which He did with one stroke of His Word alone. He trampled on them with the fierceness of the wrath of the Almighty God, bloodying them to a pulp.

Then with His sword, He stabbed the Beast and the Roman devil through their human hearts, holding them up in the air with one hand. He ordered the gates of Hell to be opened up and He flung the two devils into the Lake of Eternal Lava where the flames of vengeance will scourge them relentlessly for all eternity. They will pay for the blood of millions of God's people on their hands and for the evil they'd let loose on Earth.

Soon after, the Son of Man called on their leader, Satan,

who had been hiding in the shadows all along, hiding behind his treachery and deceit.

The Son of Man with the power of His Word, launched Satan into a bottomless chasm where he will await the time when he too will join the Beast and the Roman devil in the Lake of Eternal Lava.

As many of you witnessed, while these events came to pass, all mortals on Earth and in Limbo waited to be judged. The ones who the Son of Man forgave were escorted to Heaven with archangel Kerim and Cristal, the human warrior known for shutting down Purgatory.

With the help of the archangels and His army, the Son of Man destroyed the Jerusalem of the Earth, the place where He had been nailed to a cross.

With His Divine Power, the Son of Man has built a new Jerusalem, the Jerusalem of Heaven, the true city of peace, where the descendants of Abraham, the ones whose sins were forgiven by Him, will live together in peace for eternity.

⊗⊗⊗

A LOUD APPLAUSE BROKE OUT AND EVERYONE LEAPT TO their feet.

The archangels gave Mikail a hearty smack on the back while the crowd roared.

"Not bad at all," Raffe said. "You can do the opening speech at the feast tonight."

Mikail gave a small smile. "I respectfully decline."

"But Prophets Abraham, Moses, Mohammad will be there. We'll make sure the Almighty knows how well you did today."

REVEAL

SERENA GAVE HARRY A KISS ON THE CHEEK.

"You finally finished the last book in the trilogy," she said.

They were on a short trip to Earth, accompanying Raffe on a mission to help rebuild cities in what once was Israel.

"Fresh off the 3D printer," he said holding up the book.

It felt surreal to be on Earth where the technology he had built was still holding up. The world had taken a step backwards where the remaining humans were doing things old school. They lived life in small communities similar to a kibbutz, growing their own food, and taking care of each other.

The Son of Man ruled the world but He did so by watching from above. Raffe said, He wasn't a micromanager and preferred his angels and now souls like him to help guide His people.

Serena finished updating the Truth Seeker blog with the latest updates.

"Is there any traffic on the server?" she asked.

He checked the server logs and almost fell off the chair. "We've got five thousand new subscribers since the last time we were here."

She grinned. "Raffe did open interranet cafés in the major towns as you suggested. Why are you surprised that interest in your blog has gone up? Especially since your website is the only one on the interranet."

He chuckled, letting her punch him in the arm.

She said, "We better get going. Raffe's not going to be pleased we've gone over the clock on our lunch break again."

She jumped off the stool, pulled open the door and stepped outside into the sunshine.

"I just love how clean the air is!" she cried, spinning around with her arms out.

Humanity had been saved from ultimate doom and knowing that he and Serena played a little part in that made him proud.

And with that thought, he logged off the terminal, walked out from the café onto the street and joined his wife, breathing in the balmy air.

Dear Reader,

It has been quite a journey and I couldn't have done it without your support. Thank you for reading my books.

If you enjoyed reading Reveal, please take a few minutes to submit a review on GoodReads and the store where the book was purchased. As an independent author, your support helps me get my work in the hands of readers like you. I appreciate each and every review.

I have plans for a new novel in the near future and hope you will follow me on my social media platforms.

For more information about my other books and film projects, visit my blog at http://www.anne-raevasquez.com or send me a tweet @write2film.

Till our paths cross again,
Anne-Rae Vasquez
Truth Seekers unite!

ACKNOWLEDGMENTS

A very big **thank you** to my wonderful beta readers! Their commitment and dedication has helped Reveal be the best it can be.

Extra recognition and thanks to Josefina Rosado, Lauren Stoolfire, Bishop Wong and Danklerr Benadam who went over *Reveal* page by page, chapter by chapter with a fine tooth comb. I am grateful for their meticulous attention to detail, flagging inconsistencies and issues with the storyline. Their constructive feedback was extremely invaluable and no words can describe my heartfelt gratitude.

Thank you to my dear beta readers, multiplied by a billion. I appreciate your loyal companionship through this very long journey together.

Speaking of journey, I've been dreaming of a new novel and hope you will join me for the next round. ;)

Anne-Rae Vasquez

ABOUT THE AUTHOR

Anne-Rae Vasquez's latest novels are Doubt, Resist and Reveal from the Among Us Trilogy, Gold winner of the Readers' Favorite Book Awards. The Among Us Trilogy questions what is beyond the reality of this world and ties in different supernatural religious beliefs of God, Heaven, Purgatory and Hell, angels and demons apocalypse, spirituality and fantasy by mixing themes from shows like Fringe and Supernatural to create an end of the world religious paranormal mystery thriller.

Her previous novel Almost a Turkish Soap Opera was adapted into a screenplay and later produced into an award winning feature film and web series and was her directorial debut. Her other works include: Gathering Dust - a collection of poems, Salha's Secrets to Middle Eastern Cooking Cookbook and Teach Yourself Great Web Design in a Week, published by Sams.net (a division of Macmillan Publishing).

In her parallel life, she hosts/produces Fiction Frenzy TV, a VLog channel featuring indie artists, authors, filmmakers and musicians. In addition to this, she is a freelances journalist for Blasting News (and previously Digital Journal).

To find out more, visit:

www.anne-raevasquez.com

LIST OF CHARACTERS

Harry Doubt – 24-year-old former child prodigy; Operations Manager for Global Nation by day; by night he is trying to find out why his mother and other parents of child prodigies were kidnapped by Global Nation in the Middle East. He is the programmer who designed and created "Truth Seekers", a popular online virtual reality game with over a million players. Changed his last name from "Doub" to "Doubt" after his father passed away stating he was never really a father to him anyway; has dual Israeli and American citizenship.

Cristal Hernandez – 24-year-old former child prodigy, graduated from Global Nation University with Harry Doubt at 19 years with a PhD in Computer Sciences, not religious but had a Catholic upbringing; book smart but doubts herself; just realized she has special powers and is learning to control them; fell in love with Kerim before finding out he was an angel; learned that God had sent Archangel Rafael to destroy her because her powers could open the portals to the spiritual worlds, Limbo, Purgatory, Heaven and Hell.

Serena Keensky – athletic, teaches self-defense at Global Nation, has a black belt in several forms of martial arts including Krav Maga; is an avid Truth Seeker gamer; lived in many places around the world, the last being in the Philippines where her father is the ambassador for Russia; is a no-nonsense person.

Gabriel Windam – top player of the Truth Seekers online virtual reality game; loves the 70's era; loyal to Harry; was killed by accident trying to protect Kerim; doesn't realize he's dead.

Kerim Ilgaz – was hired to provide Security to GN by Harry; served in the Turkish army for four years prior to that; was revealed that he was a guardian angel; has feelings for Cristal; reported to Raffe (aka Archangel Rafael) until he fell.

Raffe (aka Archangel Rafael) – when in human form is an abrasive, tough Israeli; in angelic form is a formidable power; has a strange sense of humor; was on a mission to destroy Cristal.

Aaron Doub – Harry's father, famous GN Physicist who died right before he was able to prove the theory of time travel; was never close to his son; loved his wife Bina but always put his work ahead of his family; has Israeli and American citizenship.

Bina Schwartz – Harry's mother; Israeli wife and mother; denied her spirituality until she was kidnapped by GN demon scientists for the soul separation experiments; her soul escaped to Limbo with the soul of Carlos Hernadez, Cristal's father.

Saeed Nariman – GN Physicist and assistant to Aaron

Doub; sold his soul to a demon; had been Bina and Harry's confidante and friend.

Shelley Lionheart – president of Global Nation University and charitable organization with headquarters around the world.

Dr. Sarah Goldberg - psychiatrist; was in charge of testing Cristal during her incarceration at GN Tel Aviv

Joanna Chan - One of Truth Seekers top gamer; was recruited to take the game offline to search for her missing father. During their first encounters Cristal found her annoying.

General Assaf or Abu Walid - father of Walid, works at Global Nation Tel Aviv and is the president's trusted generals. Mysterious and short tempered.

Im Walid - mother of Walid, lives in Megiddo with her two sons and three young daughters. Strong, loving and kind.

Walid - resident of Megiddo, he met Cristal and Harry in Akko when the big earthquake occurred. Kerim entrusted him to watch over Cristal right after.

Bezel - the devil. When Cristal caused the earthquake, it opened the portals to Heaven, Limbo and Hell. The devil left Hell and possessed Israeli Agent Yaffa Bauer's body and swallowed Aaron Doub's soul which backfired when Cristal performed an exorcism.

Yaffa Bauer - Special Israeli National Security Agent; suspected Kerim was a terrorist and inadvertently shot and killed Gabriel during an altercation before the big earthquake.

RECAP OF BOOK 1

Former child prodigies, Harry Doubt and Cristal Hernandez both earned their PhD's and went to work together for Global Nation University. Harry, a young and brilliant programmer is the son of a famous quantum physicist (Aaron) who died during an after-work dinner party. His father's theories about time travel were controversial. Aaron's business partner, Dr. Saeed, was also a famous experimental scientist. His mother, Bina, disappeared while volunteering on a peace-keeping mission in Palestine.

Harry developed *Truth Seekers*, an online virtual reality game. He began hiring all the best programmers and game players he could find. They all had a mission to find out what was behind the scenes of certain mysterious events. And with the development of the story we learn that some members of this team have some special abilities that are not completely natural.

Cristal is capable of producing earthquakes, although she

is afraid of her powers and is not sure how they work or how to control them. During an emotional event, she caused a major earthquake, which simultaneously hit many different cities in the world.

Kerim, hired as security by Harry and who later becomes Cristal's boyfriend, is capable of reading her mind. However, things are not as they appear.

The Truth Seekers find some portals that they believe to be entrances for wormholes for time travelling. They go to Israel to research one of those portals. But not everyone in Harry's team, such as Serena and Gabriel, know what is going on and what his motivations to plan his missions are. It turns out he wants to look for his father and mother. Mystery and intrigue cause turbulence in the relationship among the members of Harry's team. And during a persecution from the Israeli Secret Service to capture Kerim, Gabriel is shot and killed.

Harry, Cristal and Serena soon find out that Kerim had been posing as a human but really was a secret agent of God. His memories as an angel had been temporarily suppressed when he had accepted the mission explaining why Kerim, believing that he was human, had fallen in love with Cristal going against God's rule where *angels and humans are not allowed to be physically involved with each other*. Becoming completely human meant that Kerim could complete his mission on Earth undetected by GN demons. His mission from God was to infiltrate GN and prevent Cristal from opening the portals to the Spiritual worlds no matter what it took.

Dr. Saeed reveals that he is possessed by a demon and tries to overcome Cristal so that he can enter the portal.

Raffe, a strange friend of Kerim, reveals he is the Archangel Rafael sent by God to destroy Cristal if Kerim can't stop her from opening the portals.

When Cristal's powers are unleashed in Akko, Israel, the site of what they thought was a wormhole; her powers inadvertently rip open a portal to Limbo. Harry steps into the portal, promising her that he will find her father and his mother and bring them back to Earth.

Archangel Rafael orders Kerim to kill Cristal. Kerim defies the orders and brings her to safety. Before Kerim flies into the heavens, he commands Walid, a resident of Megiddo, to protect Cristal. Megiddo is also known as Armageddon.